The Staff and the Orb

Book II of

He Walks With Dragons

Stanley S. Thornton

Published by

Mystic Dragon Publishing
3519 Cosbey Avenue
Baldwin Park, California 91706

Copyright © 2013 Stanley S. Thornton

All rights reserved

ISBN: 978-0-9889989-3-3 (hc)
ISBN: 978-0-9889989-4-0 (sc)
ISBN: 978-0-9889989-5-7 (e)

LCCN: 2014904752

Cover Art by Jason Thornsberry

ACKNOWLEDGEMENTS

    First, I would like to thank my editor, Gary Klinga, for helping to turn this work into a finished piece of writing. Secondly, I wish to thank the characters from Book I for pushing me to complete this book. Without their constant meddling, incessant nagging and shameless whining, I would not have been able to finish this book. Yet in all honesty, I cannot blame them for their impudence. After all, this is their story.

TABLE OF CONTENTS

Chapter 1: **The Long Journey Home**   1

Chapter 2: **The Farmer Takes a Wife**   49

Chapter 3: **A Dragon is Born**   85

Chapter 4: **The Secret Revealed**   117

Chapter 5: **No Such Thing as Immortality**   151

Chapter 6: **The Darkness Defeated**   183

Chapter 7: **Returned to the Fold**   217

Poems   239

Chapter 1

The Long Journey Home

Draig leaned against the makeshift memorial in the middle of the freshly dug graveyard and watched his companions make their way down the side of the mountain and wander off in the direction of their own choosing. One by one, in their own turn they grew smaller and smaller as they moved further away until eventually disappearing from his sight.

After standing alone and lost in thought for quite some time, Draig picked up his armor and walked over to Onyxia. He tied the armor to the back of her saddle and draped a blanket over the armor to conceal it from sight. He picked up his wildcat, Lucky and placed her at the front of the saddle and then climbed into the saddle. Lucky proudly assumed her position as lookout.

Draig looked to the freshly dug graves of his fallen comrades. He then took a long look down into the valley below. His attention was brought back to the makeshift memorial they had constructed and he thought aloud as he scanned the graves.

"It is fitting that you should overlook the place where you gave your lives defending our way of life. Your sacrifice was not in vain as our brothers were able to escape."

Draig turned to ride away, but before he had ridden ten paces, he stopped and turned quietly around. As he sat there on Onyxia, he took one last look at the graveyard to remember not to mourn. Draig knew that this scene was to be the last memory he would have of the life he once lived. He sat there with a sad heart and then he spoke his last words to his fallen brothers:

"Fois caraid. Thoir an aire prìseil caraid." He then spoke in a whisper, "Rest in peace, dear friends."

It was now time for him to leave the old memories behind. Draig made his way down from the side of the mountain. When he reached the road, he surveyed it carefully and then took the southern road toward the coastal town of Marseille. As it was a full two-day ride to Marseille, his journey would give him plenty of time to think about the future. The future was all that he had left.

As Draig made his way down the road, he thought about the battle and looking up toward the portal to the astral plane. He remembered the look on Draco's face as the magical door swung closed, forever separating those in this realm from those in the other. Tears welled up in his eyes and a lone tear rolled down his face. Draig knew that his world had ended when that door closed.

But this was not a time for sadness. It was a time to focus on the future. Draig could not help but reminisce about his times with Draco. He figured it was more important, at least for this one day, to think about his best friend who had that quirky sense of humor.

It was an uneventful ride the whole afternoon. He was surprised that he did not pass a single person all day. Then again, it was not as though Draig really expected to run into anyone so far north on this particular road. Still, it would have been a welcome sight to see other travelers.

As darkness approached, Draig searched for a nice place to camp for the night. Finding a small clearing to the side of the road with a nice tree in the middle, he loosed Onyxia's saddle and dropped it to the ground next to the tree. While Onyxia grazed, Draig collected dried branches to make a comfy fire.

Draig brought his palms together and drew the treoir into his palms. He let the treoir form a ball of energy between his palms. The ball of energy became an orb of fire. He then tossed the fiery orb into the middle of the fire circle. There was a flash of flame and the pieces of wood burst into flame.

Draig scrounged around in his bags for a piece of bread and a bottle of wine. Meantime, Lucky came running up with a mouse in her mouth. Draig looked down and laughed.

"That's all right, Lucky. You do not have to share. You can keep the whole mouse for yourself."

Lucky proudly pranced over to the fire and contently consumed her supper. Draig sat down next to her to eat his piece of bread and drink a cup of wine. He looked at his two friends and thought how lonely it would be with just the three of them, but they would have to learn to accept things as they are now.

When they finished their meal Draig lay down using the saddle as a pillow. Lucky curled up against his side and Onyxia wandered over next to the tree so as to be with her friends. As the fire dwindled Draig closed his eyes and went to sleep.

Draig's dreams were filled with memories from the past. He dreamt about when he was in his village as a young boy. He dreamt about when he found Lucky and begged to keep her. He dreamt about finding Onyxia and training her. He also dreamt of the battle and seeing Draco's face as the door swung closed. As the night wore on

Draig continued to relive memories from his past. In the middle of the night, Draig woke up in a cold sweat and screaming:

"Get out of my head! You are all talking at once, I cannot understand you! Please, get out of my head!"

Draig knelt in the darkness with his sword in his outstretched hand. His heart was pounding in his chest and sweat was pouring from his face. As he scanned the darkness, expecting to see someone lurking just beyond his sight, he came to realize it was all just a dream.

His hand trembled as he lowered his sword. He was visibly shaken by a dream filled with many voices all shouting at him at once. Though he could hear voices, yet he could not see anyone. After a while, Draig shook off the strange dream and managed to complete his night's rest without further complications.

In the morning Draig saddled up and ventured forth to Marseille. The morning's journey proved uneventful. At midday, Draig sat down and leaned against a tree trunk for a rest. Onyxia grazed here and there, never getting very far away from Draig. As Draig was enjoying the warmth of the sun that broke through the branches of the trees towering over him, he looked down the long road ahead and caught sight of a man and a child walking toward him in the distance. He immediately began wondering who the pair might be, but at that distance he could barely make them out. As he waited for them to approach, Lucky climbed into his lap and Onyxia continued to graze.

As the pair drew near, Draig was able to make out the distinct features of the man and child. The man was tall and muscular. His graying hair reached down to his neck, and the age lines on his face showed his advanced years. He wore a dark brown robe and carried a large walking stick that suggested he was either a monk or a friar. The child was a young boy of about ten or eleven. He had short, dark brown hair, and he had the appearance as if someone placed a bowl upon his head as a guide to cut his hair. He was timid and kept his head down, his eyes always looking at the ground. He would only occasionally look up.

"Good day," said Draig. "It is a good day for travelling."

"Good day, good sir," the old man said. "May blessings be upon you on your journey."

"I am Draig, and I would be pleased to have you share a midday meal with me." Draig whistled to Onyxia.

"I am Jerrod, and this is my young apprentice, Paul," said the old man.

Draig noticed a sense of caution in Jerrod's voice. It was obvious to Draig that Jerrod was hiding something. He pretended not to notice since he reasoned that it could be nothing more than being cautious with a stranger.

Draig fiddled around in a large sack that was tied to the side of the saddle. He pulled out two pieces of meal bread and loosened a water skin that was hanging on the saddle. He handed one of the pieces of bread to Jerrod and placed the water skin on the ground between them. Jerrod tore the bread in half, handing the boy a piece before sitting down on a fallen log.

To Draig's amazement, the boy took a silk napkin from his sleeve and laid it on a small boulder before sitting down. Draig also paid attention to the manner in which the boy ate. Paul sat with his feet together and his knees touching. He rested his elbows on his thighs as he picked small pieces from the bread with his fingers and slowly chewed each piece.

Draig continued to quietly study the pair as they ate. Draig was aware that the old man was concealing a sword beneath his robe. Normally, a concealed sword would mean very little, but it was no secret that monks did not carry swords. With his curiosity piqued, Draig began to guide the conversation.

"How come you to be on the road this day?" asked Draig.

"We are on a pilgrimage to the north."

"I am on a sort of pilgrimage myself, more or less."

"Where does your pilgrimage take you, my friend?" asked Jerrod.

Draig thought carefully. "I do not know yet. My future beckons to me from somewhere beyond. For now I travel to Marseille. It is as good a place as any to begin."

"Where are you from, my friend?" Draig inquired.

"Just now we come from Marseille," Jerrod answered.

Draig became increasingly interested in Jerrod's body language as they continued to chat. Jerrod appeared a bit anxious. First he looked south along the road where they came and then glanced north along the road where they are heading. He also scanned the forest as if he was looking for something.

At this point Draig began seriously sizing up this paranoid monk trying to figure out who he really was. Draig looked closely at Jerrod's hands. It did not take much effort to realize that these were not the hands of a monk. It became so obvious that Draig felt the need to speak up:

"Those are not the hands of a man that prays."

"Pardon me, sir?" Jerrod replied, quickly hiding his hands.

"When you have observed life as long as I have," Draig responded, "you begin to see things as they are and not as they appear. As I said, those are not the hands of a man that prays. They are the hands of a warrior, and you carry a sword concealed beneath your robe."

Jerrod became even more nervous than before. A look of fear came over his face like that of a trapped animal. He slid his hand into his robe and grasped the hilt of his sword. Draig realized he had upset his guest and that he had better to say something fast to diffuse the situation.

"There is nothing to fear," Draig said. "I am but a traveler on the road and nothing more."

As Jerrod removed his hand from his sword. "You do not speak like a mere traveler on the road."

"It is not so much," Draig offered. "There are many things a man can see if he opens his mind. Even a blind man can tell you if the sun is shining on his face or the rain falls on his head."

Jerrod was already becoming more suspicious of Draig's observations. After all, when travelling on the road, you learn to be friendly to strangers you meet along the way but not too overly trusting. Draig had come dangerously close to crossing that line of trust, and that is the exact moment when Draig took that last step too far.

"I could not help but wonder if Paul is your granddaughter?"

Jerrod leaped to his feet and drew his sword. That was when Draig realized that he had asked one question too many. Draig tried to calm him down. "Be at ease, friend. I mean no harm. I was simply curious why you would pretend she was a boy, nothing more."

As Jerrod sheathed his sword, "This is Princess Paulette and I am her bodyguard."

"But why do you disguise her as a boy?"

"She is disguised so that we can remain in the shadows unseen."

"If I can tell she's a girl, I am sure others can."

"We do not usually get close enough to people for them to notice."

"But surely there will come a day when she can no longer pass as a boy."

Jerrod then explained. "By that time she will no longer need to hide, but that is a rather long story."

"I am not going anywhere at the moment. My horse, Onyxia, is still grazing. I have time for a long explanation, not to mention that you have piqued my curiosity."

"Her parents were killed when she was very young. She is still too young to lay claim to the throne. The chancellor rules in her stead until she comes of age, but there are rumors that the chancellor does not wish to abdicate the throne. Therefore, we travel incognito on the chance that the chancellor tries to prevent her coming of age."

Draig thought about the situation for a moment. He whistled for Onyxia, who trotted to him. Draig then fiddled in a large sack tied to Onyxia's saddle. He pulled five shiny gold coins from the sack and walked up to Paulette.

As he held out the coins to her he said, "I have little to offer a princess. Please take these coins as a tribute to the one who shall be queen."

Paulette looked to Jerrod, as she had no idea what she should do. Jerrod nodded and she took the coins that Draig offered.

"Thank you, Draig. I am honored by your gift," she said.

"Thank you for your contribution, Draig," Jerrod said. "Your kindness will be remembered."

Draig mounted Onyxia and called down to his lunch guests. "I wish good fortune follows you on your journey. Princess, I wish you a long and just reign. May you find happiness all of the days of your life."

With the pleasantries over, Draig pointed Onyxia's nose toward Marseille and continued his trek to the sea. It was late morning when Draig came upon a wagon on the side of the road. The wagon was facing north and the wagoner was sitting on the ground nearby. The wagoner was tall and muscular, obviously from lifting freight all day. He had blonde hair and dark eyes. He was just sitting there with his head in his hands.

As Draig approached, Lucky raised herself up on all fours and bobbed her head up and down. She was carefully examining the situation, but for what she had no idea. Draig called down to the wagoner. "Good day, sir, you appear to be having a problem."

Without even looking up, he answered, "I have a broken wheel and there is no way I can fix it alone."

The wagoner let out a long sigh. He then rose and walked around to the side of the wagon and stood staring at the broken wheel. He simply shook his head, knowing that there was no way he was going to be able to fix the wheel without help.

He turned his head and took a long look down the road. In reality, he was wishing that a Roman patrol would wander by and offer to assist him, but he had no such luck. He knew it would take at least three or four strong men to lift the side of the wagon, but he was having nothing but bad luck.

"May I be of assistance to you?" asked Draig.

The wagoner threw up his arms in defeat and said, "Unless you can pull a couple more people out of thin air, I'm going to have to say that there is very little you can do."

Never having owned a wagon, Draig really knew very little about repairing one, but he also knew that he could not just leave the man stranded on the side of the road. He looked into the wagon and saw a long length of rope. He looked up to see a large tree limb stretching out over the road. Draig's mind was already starting to put together a plan when he noticed a large, heavy branch lying on the ground just a few yards from the road.

Draig asked, "What if I could solve the physical part of the problem?"

"It would be fairly easy in that case," the wagoner explained. "The men would lift this side of the wagon. At that time I would slide a barrel under the bottom of the wagon so that the wheel would be off the ground. Finally, I would remove the wheel, fix it and then put it back on."

"You fetch me that strong branch over there and I will get the wagon lifted."

"I told you it would take three or four men to lift that wagon!" the wagoner insisted.

"You get the branch," Draig said with a smile, "and I will lift the wagon. Trust me."

The wagoner shook his head but went to get the branch anyway. Draig pulled a barrel from the wagon and set it on the ground next to the broken wheel. After climbing into the wagon, Draig picked up the rope and tossed one end over the tree limb. He tied one end to the axle of the wagon, wrapped the other end around the trunk of the tree and tied it to Onyxia's saddle.

As the wagoner came out of the woods dragging a large branch behind him, he said, "Here is your branch. Now what are you up to?"

Draig slid the branch under the wagon and cinched up on the branch until it was tight against the bottom of the wagon.

Draig whistled and called out: "Onyxia, pull!"

Onyxia started to slowly move forward. As the rope became taut, Draig started pushing up on the branch. Slowly the side of the wagon began to rise. When the side of the wagon rose enough to take the wheel off the ground,

Draig whistled and called out: "Onyxia, halt!"

The wagoner slid the barrel under the wagon, and once again Draig whistled and called out: "Onyxia, back!"

Onyxia then began to slowly walk backwards until the wagon rested on the barrel. Onyxia stopped, and Draig laid the branch down to help the wagoner work on the broken wheel.

The wagoner removed the pin and pulled the wheel off the axle. Draig fed Onyxia a crabapple as the wagoner fixed the wheel. The wagoner brought the wheel around into position, and Draig lifted the branch until it again came into contact with the bottom of the wagon. Onyxia began walking forward until the wagon lifted off the barrel. The wagoner pulled the barrel out from under the wagon and both slowly lowered the wagon until it was once again on the ground.

Draig untied the rope and returned it to the wagon as the wagoner removed the branch from the road. The wagoner then held out a couple coins to Draig.

"Thank you, friend. I could not have fixed this wheel without your help."

Draig responded, "Keep your coins. You owe me nothing. I would not be the man I am if I did not assist someone in trouble."

The wagoner smiled and put away his coins. "Once again, thank you for your assistance."

The wagoner climbed back into his wagon and headed north. Draig climbed back into the saddle and resumed his journey to the sea.

He passed few people during the rest of the afternoon, but those he did merely smiled and waved. For the most part he simply talked to Onyxia and Lucky to pass the time. As night approached, Draig could see Marseille in the distance. It was a welcome sight, though it was still far enough away that it would have to wait for tomorrow. Draig estimated he would arrive in Marseille just before midday.

Draig unsaddled Onyxia and placed the saddle against a tree. He then gathered stones and built a small fire circle before collecting small pieces of wood for a fire. He looked around to make sure that no one was nearby. Draig brought his palms together and drew the treoir into his palms. He let the treoir form a ball of energy between his palms. The ball of energy became an orb of fire. He then tossed the fiery orb into the middle of the fire circle. The orb flashed and the pieces of wood burst into flame.

Draig leaned against his saddle and made himself comfortable just as a man with a handcart filled with baskets of vegetables came strolling up. The man was short and stout, with brown hair and just a whisper of a mustache. His clothing suggested he was a local farmer. The man bowed to Draig.

"Good evening, sire. I dread being alone on this road at night. Would you welcome some company on this evening?"

"Good evening," Draig said, "You are more than welcome to join my companions and me."

"Companions?" the man asked as he looked around.

Rising to his feet, he said, "I am called Draig." He pointed to his horse. "This is Onyxia. Though she does not talk much, she is a very good listener." He held up Lucky and said, "And this sweet thing is Lucky. While she is a most beautiful cat, I'm afraid she is not as good a hunter as she thinks she is."

"I am pleased to meet you and your companions," the man responded. "I am Francois from Avignon. I am a farmer on my way to Marseille to sell my crops."

Francois walked over to his cart and pulled out a pot and gathered some of his vegetables. He returned to the campfire and began preparing a simple vegetable stew. It was then that Lucky came wandering up with a mouse in her mouth and dropped it next to Francois and stared up at him. Francois looked at Draig, not knowing what he was supposed to do or say.

"It is a generous offer," Draig said to Lucky, "but it is not enough meat for all of us. I suggest you enjoy the mouse while Francois and I settle for the stew."

Lucky picked up her mouse and sat next to the saddle to eat it. Francois and Draig sat near the fire to eat their stew. After eating, the two men settled in for a night of rest. Lucky snuggled up against Draig's leg while Onyxia wandered around nearby. It was a nice setting to get to chew the fat while they digested their supper.

"What brings you to Marseille?" Francois asked.

"It seemed as good a place as any to begin." Draig replied.

"To begin? Marseille is not your final destination?"

"My fate waits for me out there," Draig said. "I hear it calling to me, but I do not know where it is."

"So, you have no idea where you are going?"

"Well, I have seen enough of the Roman Empire. I would like to get as far away from Rome as I can get."

"Well, I would suggest that you consider the Isle of Britannia," Francois suggested. "While the Romans are also there, their presence is less noticeable than elsewhere, and it is not like you can travel any farther west than that."

While Francois would have no way of knowing, Draig could tell him from personal knowledge that Britannia is definitely not the farthest west one can go, but this was not the time or place to have that discussion.

Draig thought about what Francois had said, and he was right about one thing. Draig had made enough trips to Britannia to know that the Roman presence was more limited and was less formally structured than other places.

"I suppose you are right," Draig said as he rolled over to go to sleep.

Draig and Francois slept comfortably as the fire slowly wavered, flickered and died out. In the middle of the night the calm was suddenly broken as Draig woke up in a cold sweat just as he had the night before.

"You are all talking at once . . . I cannot understand you! Stop it! Leave me alone!"

The commotion woke Francois from his sound sleep. He found Draig kneeling with his sword in his hand and sweat dripping from his brow. Draig slowly lowered his sword and began weeping.

"They would not stop talking. They were all talking at once."

Francois reached out and put his hand on Draig and shook him gently. "Draig, are you all right?"

"Yes, Francois. I guess it was a dream. There were all of these voices calling out to me at once, and I could not understand any of them."

Assured that Draig was all right, Francois returned to a blissful sleep. Draig, on the other hand, sat up for a while to try to regain his composure. He was uneasy, having had the same dream two nights in a row. He wondered if they were simply nightmares or something more.

Draig finally decided that there was little purpose to continue focusing on the dream. He closed his eyes and finally returned to sleep. The rest of the night passed without incident, and the rising sun brought the pair of travelers a warm, sunny morning.

Draig saddled Onyxia, bid Francois farewell and continued his ride toward Marseille. His thoughts turned to Britannia. He had made many trips to Britannia over the years, and it was home to the great circle of stones of which he was familiar.

When Draig finally arrived in Marseille, he sat at the edge of town and simply watched the activity going on about him. People were rushing from shop to shop and children were playing in the streets. Draig always enjoyed large towns as there was so much more to experience, and Marseille's thousand residents certainly qualified.

Regardless, there was no time for window shopping or spending time drinking in a tavern. Draig could ill afford wasting time as he knew if he dawdled too much in town, he might miss catching a trade ship headed for Britannia. He made only one stop to buy a couple loaves of fresh bread and a small supply of fresh fruit.

When Draig arrived at the docks, he wasted no time trying to locate a ship bound for Britannia. He did not want to risk missing a ship and having to stay the night in Marseille. So, as Draig walked the docks, he called out to every dockhand.

"Is there a ship sailing for Britannia today?"

He had little luck at first, but it did not take long before he heard a voice call back to him:

"Captain Arimah sails for Chichester Harbour on the hour as he needs but to load a little more cargo before he sails."

Draig knew that Chichester Harbour was in southern Britannia and that it would be but a short distance to travel from the port to the circle of stones. He turned and spotted the person who called out. He was a scruffy, old dockhand, tall and muscular. He had dark brown hair, but there were traces of gray that indicated he was no longer a young man. He had a large scar above his right eye and several scars across his arms that suggested that he had experienced battle.

Draig asked courteously, "Which ship would belong to Captain Arimah, may I ask?"

The dockhand pointed. "That is his ship over there. The captain is standing there."

Draig looked to where the dockhand pointed and saw the captain—a tall, white skin man with red hair and blue eyes—standing next to a trade ship. Even if he had not worn his tunic and sandals, Draig would have still been able to easily identify him as a Phoenician.

It was intriguing to Draig to find a Phoenician in Marseille, especially since Phoenicia had been invaded and conquered such a very long time ago. It was as if Captain Arimah had somehow stepped out of the past and into the present, but that would be true of Draig as well.

Intrigued or not, this was not the time to stand around wondering about trivial things. It would not be long before Captain Arimah and his ship would be setting sail.

As Draig walked up, Captain Arimah smiled and said, "Good day, friend. How may I be of help to you?"

Draig reached into a large sack tied to Onyxia's saddle and pulled out five shiny gold coins. Turning to Captain Arimah, Draig held out the gold coins in the palm of his hand. He made a simple demand of the captain.

"I am Draig, and I wish to purchase passage to Britannia for me and my two companions, no questions asked."

Captain Arimah gave Draig a good looking over and then gave Onyxia and Lucky a good looking over. He then looked back at Draig. Without even thinking he just could not help himself.

"What takes you to Britannia, my friend?"

Draig stood there silently for a moment. He took one of the coins from his hand and returned it to the sack. He then held out the four gold coins in the palm of his hand and made the same simple demand once more.

"I wish to purchase passage to Britannia for me and my two companions, no questions asked."

Captain Arimah would not be a captain if he failed to catch the meaning of what Draig was saying. He smiled at Draig and took the coins.

"As you wish, my friend," Captain Arimah said. "Take yourselves aboard. We depart within the hour."

Draig led Onyxia aboard the trade ship while Captain Arimah stood there staring at the four shiny gold coins that sat in the palm of his hand. In his travels Captain Arimah had seen every coin ever minted. It was no secret to him where these coins originated. These gold coins were from the isle of Crete and he was well aware of it.

Captain Arimah also knew that Crete had been conquered by Rome a long time ago. This begged the question: Where did this stranger come by these coins when Rome had melted down Crete's coins to make Roman coins? While he was very curious about how his passenger came by these coins, such things would have to wait. Preparing his ship to set sail was much more important.

Draig led Onyxia to a quiet place on the deck so as to be out of way of the crew. Making sure that the blanket remained snugly wrapped around his armor, Draig slowly lowered it down from the saddle. He then removed his sword from the saddle and slid it carefully beneath the blanket. He then loosed the saddle from Onyxia's back and lowered it down and placed it next to his armor. Once the saddle was safely on deck, Lucky took up her favorite position at the front of the saddle and quickly fell asleep.

Draig looked around the deck to see who was paying notice of his actions. It appeared to Draig that none of the crew took much interest in him or what he was doing. After all, the crew was fully immersed in their chores. He then sat down and leaned against the saddle.

While Draig had done his best to hide his armor with the blanket, the fact that he had armor did not go unnoticed by the crew. The sailors on this ship were just as curious about passengers as any new crew member. They simply did not make it so obvious to the subjects of their curiosity.

Draig's sword was equally noticed by the crew. While owning a sword does not usually tell you all that much about the man who carries it, the fact that Draig's sword was of such high quality did pique the crew's interest more than usual.

Draig kept to himself all afternoon, speaking only to Onyxia and Lucky. The crew found it entertaining to watch Draig talk to his pets. As Draig talked, both Onyxia and Lucky looked at him very intensely. It was as if they could understand every word he was saying, and they seemed to hang on his every word.

The whispers began to grow as the afternoon wore on. The crew usually had little reason to be curious about passengers, but this passenger was definitely different from the usual passenger. Though their tasks had priority, it did not stop the crew from catching glimpses of Draig and his pets.

As evening approached, Captain Arimah ordered a crewman to bring up a bag of oats from the hold for Onyxia. As the crew member set the oats down in front of Onyxia, he looked at Lucky as she sat on the saddle.

"Is there anything in particular that your littlest friend would prefer to eat?"

Draig reached out and scratched Lucky behind her ear. "Other than the occasional mouse or bird that she manages to catch, she eats what I eat. She would have it no other way.

"Your supper will be here in a moment," the crewman said as he walked away.

It was only a few minutes later when Captain Arimah approached, carrying two bowls. "I hope you do not mind the company. It is my duty as captain to share an evening meal with my passengers."

"What kind of guest would I be if I refused such an honor?" Draig responded. "I would be pleased to share a meal with my host."

Captain Arimah handed a bowl to Draig and sat down. Draig reached into a bag on his saddle and pulled out a piece of meal bread. He broke it in half and offered half to his host. The bowls were filled with a crude stew of vegetables with a bit of meat mixed in.

For every few bits that Draig took, Lucky would stick her nose into the bowl and grab a small bite for herself. Sometimes it was a piece of meat and sometimes it was a piece of vegetable. It did not matter to her which it was as long as she was eating what Draig was eating.

While they continued to eat their meal, Draig's curiosity began to get the better of him. It is not every day that he is in the presence of a Phoenician who might be contemplating his fate.

"So, how is it that I am able to sit here in the presence of a Phoenician?" Draig asked.

Captain Arimah simply smiled and rubbed his thumb across the tips of his fingers. Draig knew exactly what this action meant. He reached into his sack and pulled out a single gold coin and handed it over to Captain Arimah. As Captain Arimah continued to pick at his stew, he explained:

"My ancestor, after who I am named, was at sea when the Persians invaded our homeland. Unable to return home to a free Phoenicia, he did as so many others and fled to Carthage. Though our homeland was gone, we remained Phoenicians. To protect our blood lines, our ancestors gathered together in one section of Carthage. As my ancestors had all been sea traders, I naturally followed their example and became a sea trader as well. Unfortunately, it is a sad fact that there are fewer of us with the passing of every day."

Draig looked up at Captain Arimah with sadness in his eyes and said, "I know how you feel. Honestly, I do."

Unknown to Captain Arimah, Draig knew exactly how he felt. Just as it was with Captain Arimah so it was with him. Looking at Arimah was very much like looking into a mirror as there also were fewer of Draig's kind.

While their situations were very different, their fates were the same. It brought back old memories that caused sadness within Draig. Yet, he would have to hide his sadness because it would not be easy to explain his sadness without exposing the secrets of his past.

After they finished their meager supper, Captain Arimah went and fetched a large cask of Phoenician wine. He placed it in front of Draig. He then held out two large cups and grinned at his guest.

"No meal would be complete without a few cups of Phoenician wine!"

Draig took one of the cups from Captain Arimah, and the two of them drank well into the night. It did not take long before Captain Arimah was eagerly repeating stories his grandfather had related to him about life in Phoenicia.

The crew soon began to collect around the happy pair. The members of the crew loved sitting around listening to Captain Arimah's stories. They would sit in awe no matter how many times they heard the stories of his homeland. Draig enjoyed them a great deal better. The crew simply could not relate to the stories in the way Draig could.

Captain Arimah could not help feeling the growing excitement in the air as his audience grew larger. As the night wore on, Draig had enough to drink that he began telling stories of his own.

"I always found it entertaining to watch the noble visitors flocking to Tyre to purchase the famed purple dye, Tyrian purple."

"I loved the thrill of walking through the marketplace at Gebal. It is almost indescribable. He did not like shopping, so it was usually only me. It was kind of exciting and lonely at the same time."

"I miss walking the streets of Sidon and smelling the aroma of fresh baked kaak as it floated over the crowds. And one's first taste of that crunchy whole wheat bread was to die for."

Perhaps Captain Arimah simply had too much wine to drink, but something obviously kept him from recognizing that Draig was telling stories in the first person as someone who had actually walked the streets of ancient Phoenicia. Perhaps he was simply so excited to have someone to exchange stories with that he simply overlooked it.

It was also obvious that Draig had had a few sips too many because he did not catch himself. Apparently the crew was also too engrossed in the stories to have realized that Draig was speaking from personal experience and not just repeating stories.

It was finally time to bring the evening to a close. Captain Arimah would have talked all night if he could have, but even good things have to come to an end. He slowly staggered away to sleep off the night's inebriations. As Draig lay down to sleep, Lucky climbed onto his chest, curled up in a ball and went to sleep too.

In the middle of the night Draig woke up in a cold sweat and began yelling:

"Shut up! You are all talking at once . . . I cannot understand you! Please, stop talking!"

When members of the crew came running up, they found Draig on his knees with his sword in his outstretched hand and sweat dripping from his brow. Captain Arimah came running up after a few moments.

"Are you all right, my friend?"

"They will not leave me alone," Draig insisted. "They all kept talking at once, and I cannot understand them. They just kept shouting at me!"

"No one is shouting at you here, my friend. It was just a dream."

Draig slowly lowered his sword and sat there quietly for a few moments while the captain and crew watched. Finally, Draig slid his sword back under the blanket and lay back down. Soon, he was once again fast asleep.

Captain Arimah told his crew to let him be and to not speak of the events of this evening. He reasoned that Draig would not feel like being reminded of his episode. After all, do we not all have secrets that we would prefer not talk about?

Sunrise came without further incident. As Draig began to stir, he remembered the night's events and felt a sense of shame and embarrassment. While he began to stir, he made an obvious attempt at avoiding eye contact with the crew. The crew understood the reason for his behavior and did their best to not make him feel any worse than he already did.

Draig tried to keep to himself so that he did not have to talk about what happened during the night. He was also hoping to avoid having to explain the sword that he knew the whole crew had seen. Draig knew his sword was of such workmanship that it would be very difficult for Draig to explain how he came by it.

He could only hope that walking around would help put him at ease. As Draig walked up and down the deck, Lucky followed a pace behind with her head held high. Whenever a crew member would see Lucky following obediently behind, he would get the biggest smile on his face.

Draig was becoming impatient with the length of the journey. This was to be expected considering how fast Draig was used to making trips to Britannia. To be fair, he had to admit this was the first time he traveled by ship. As evening approached, a crew member brought a bag of oats for Onyxia and was soon followed by Captain

Arimah carrying two bowls of stew. He handed a bowl to Draig and then sat down.

"I apologize for the stew. When we are in port, it is easy to vary our diet. When we are at sea, however, it is much easier for us to make this simple stew."

"No need to apologize," Draig said, "While it might make a difference to the mouth, the stomach just wants to be full."

To avoid the subject of the other night, Captain Arimah moved the topic of conversation to something less traumatic for Draig:

"My crew is rather amused at how you talk to your cat and horse. It is as if you are talking to people, and they seem as if they understand you."

Draig smiled. "They understand every word I say."

"Do you have family, Draig?"

"For me, this is my family," Draig replied.

"The three of you seem inseparable," Captain Arimah said. "It is almost as if you are all pieces of a greater whole."

"I guess that in a way we are," said Draig as he gently stroked Lucky. "We started our lives following our own paths. It was Fate that caused our paths to intersect and we became one."

"I envy you, my friend," Captain Arimah said. "While I have my family and love them dearly, we will never be as close as the three of you seem to be."

"We have been together longer than you can imagine," Draig said. "If you had been together as long as we have, you too would be as close."

Intrigued, Captain Arimah asked, "How long have the three of you been together?"

Draig knew it was time to change the subject. He knew well that it would be extremely difficult to explain just how long they had been together.

"So," Draig said, "tell me about some of the places you have sailed to."

Captain Arimah talked about sailing the shores of the Great Inland Sea. He eagerly began telling stories of all the marvelous places he had been and all the sights he had seen. The more he talked, the more excited he became. It was not long before the crew began to gather. One by one, the crew began to join the conversation. Each crewman took his turn telling stories. Draig listened intently and laughed along with the crew when it was appropriate, but he did not take a turn. While the stories Draig could tell were most unique, it would also be difficult to explain certain details about them.

As it began to grow late, the crew started wandering off until only Captain Arimah remained. Then he bid Draig a good night. As Captain Arimah walked away, Draig rolled over and went to sleep with Lucky curled up next to him.

The night started very peacefully, but it did not remain so. It was not long before Draig once again woke up in a cold sweat and was once again screaming:

"Stop it! You are all talking at once! Leave me alone!"

Draig found himself standing alone on the deck, sweat dripping from his body and his sword clinched tightly in his hand. He slowly dropped to his knees and began to weep. Lucky came up to comfort him as tears rolled down Draig's face.

The crew members who were on deck hid themselves so as not to add to the situation. They remained in the shadows and could only wonder what spirits must possess poor Draig. Draig finally crawled back to his saddle.

As he lay back down he spoke softly, "Why do you not leave me alone?"

As was usual, the rest of the night passed without incident. When Draig woke he could see the shores of Britannia in the distance. While it seemed so close, it took until midday to reach the shore. Draig spent this time in solitude, making every attempt to ignore what he knew the crew must be thinking of his midnight episodes.

Upon arriving in Chichester Harbour, Draig quickly saddled Onyxia and placed Lucky in her usual place on the saddle. He quietly led Onyxia from the deck of the ship. As he climbed into the saddle, he heard Captain Arimah call to him:

"Farewell, my young friend, and may you find peace of mind in the days to come."

Draig called back: "Arimah, ragel tal-bahar, ta'l-tieghu dak l-abejett. Farewell, my old friend!"

Captain Arimah's jaw dropped. He was stunned speechless. He suspected there was more to his passenger than what he appeared, but he could not imagine where his passenger could have learned Phoenician.

Many questions swirled around in his mind as he stood on the deck and watched Draig ride away. There were still many questions but no answers for Captain Arimah as he returned to his duties. He could only resign himself to the fact that Draig would have to remain a mystery to him. Captain Arimah thought about what Draig said to him in Phoenician. "A respected man is a rich man." He thought about this and reckoned that in his case he must be a very rich man indeed.

Draig wasted no time getting out of Chichester Harbour. He made but one stop to purchase enough fresh fruit and vegetables, bread and wine to last a week or two. He did not buy meat as he thought it would be a simple enough task to obtain small amounts of meat by hunting for it himself.

Once he arrived at the outskirts of town he stopped to take one last look back toward the docks. He had enjoyed his conversations with Captain Arimah and could identify with the Phoenician's attempts to hold on to his past, but Draig sensed that his own future lay ahead, so he began his ride north.

It was just before sunset when Draig arrived at his destination. He dismounted a few paces outside the circle of stones and stood there in silence. He had forgotten how the massive bluestones towered over the plain. After a time, Draig began to walk toward the center of the stones. Onyxia and Lucky remained behind. It was almost as if they could sense that Draig needed to take this walk alone.

This was not the first time he had made this walk, but it was the first time he took this walk alone. As Draig stood at the center of the circle of stones, he suddenly realized that he did not just happen to come to this place. He was drawn to it like a moth to a flame. He did not know if he was drawn here by something from his past or by something that was waiting for him in his future. He only knew that he needed to be here.

Draig looked about at the massive bluestones that stood as cold and silent sentinels to what once was. With his eyes closed he held out his hands, palms turned toward the ground, to feel the energy that flowed beneath the ground. His spirit was filled with the ancient energy that had flowed beneath this circle of stones since the begin time.

Draig knelt and gazed intently at the stars. "Great Mother, Tiamat, have I been forsaken? Have I not kept my oath? Am I to be set upon the sea of the forgotten to drift without purpose?"

It was growing late and Draig had to make camp. Since he felt comfortable in the shadow of the circle of stones, he decided it was a good place to rest for the night. Draig removed the saddle from Onyxia and used it as a pillow. He lay down and covered himself with a blanket. Lucky climbed onto his chest, rolled up in a ball and went to sleep. Draig rested his left hand on Lucky and went to sleep as Onyxia stood nearby.

Draig woke up in the middle of the night in a cold sweat. He leapt to his feet and put his hands over his ears while Lucky hid behind the saddle and cowered in fear. Draig yelled at the top of his lungs:

"Get out of my head! You are all talking at once. . . I cannot understand you! Please, get out of my head!"

He then dropped to his knees, reached out his hands and lowered himself to the ground. There he lay and gently wept. Lucky slowly came near and began rubbing her side against Draig's leg. She could sense that something was wrong and was doing the only thing she could to comfort him.

Draig suddenly heard a voice. "Why do you tremble so, Son of Man?"

Draig reached for his sword and leapt to his feet. He held his sword out as he scanned the darkness for the source of the voice. There was nothing but silence staring back at him.

Draig called out into the darkness, "Who is there? I command you to show yourself!"

"Draig, son of Anarcher, son of Eafa, son of Eoppa, I call to you, but you do not answer."

Draig responded, "I do not understand. Who is it who calls to me?"

Just then a ghostly apparition slowly appeared in the center of the circle of stones. It was there and yet it was not there. It was faint like a memory from the past. It hovered there just above the ground. As Draig stood there staring at the apparition it spoke once more.

"I have summoned you and you have come. Do you not know me?"

Draig suddenly awoke in a cold sweat and grabbed his sword. He slowly scanned the darkness, but there was nothing there. He soon realized that all the events that had taken place during this night were but one long, eerie dream. As he wiped away the sweat from his face, he realized to whom the voice in his dream belonged.

"Draco? Is it you who calls to me in my dreams? What is it that you are trying to tell me?"

There was no answer, only silence. Draig sat there tapping his sword on the ground and trying to make sense of the dream. It was eerie enough when it was simply the same dream every night, but now it was different. Never in his life had he ever dreamt that he woke up but was still asleep, and then there was the voice. The voice was so real that he felt he could reach out and touch whoever was doing the talking.

It was not long before Draig's curiosity gave way to his need for sleep. He moved back to the saddle and made himself comfortable once more. He slowly began to drift back into the state of restful sleep.

Come first light, Draig rode eastward toward the rising sun. He rode until he reached the river Avon. There, Draig looked north along the river as he sat upon Onyxia. His eyes caught sight of a Roman hill fort in the distance. Memory told him that it was Cunetio, but he was not about to get close enough to find out for certain. As he did not want to be in close vicinity of a Roman encampment he began riding south along the shore.

He finally came upon a small clearing with a mighty oak tree towering over it. Gazing up at the tree, Draig recalled when he was a small boy in his village. He was taught that the oak tree was a good omen. It was a noble tree that had healing power; he was told, though he had to confess he did not consider such superstitions as having much relevance in his world.

"So, tell me, girl," Draig said as he patted Onyxia's neck, "do you think this is a good place to take a rest?"

With the approval of Onyxia, Draig climbed down and removed her saddle, placing it in the shade of one of the smaller trees. Lucky lay down on the saddle while Onyxia trotted around the clearing looking for a good snack. Draig took out one of the wine bottles he bought in Chichester Harbour.

As Draig lifted the bottle to his lips, he caught a glimpse of the oak tree out of the corner of his eye. He saw something that made him spit out his wine. "Draco!"

Turning to run to the tree, Draig saw there was nothing there. He knew there were no longer dragons in the world, but he was certain that he saw one standing under the tree with his wings wide open. It was so real it could not have been a dream, and it could not be the wine since he had yet to swallow any.

Draig stood there transfixed and staring at the oak tree. He finally came to the conclusion that it had to be a vision and therefore a good omen. This left no doubt in his mind that this land had to be his new home. Having decided that the oak tree would make the best shelter until he could erect some buildings, he picked up the saddle and placed it against the oak's trunk. He then sat down and thought about what buildings he needed. Obviously, he would need to build a house and also a stable so that Onyxia would have a roof over her head.

The stable that Onyxia had spent so many years living in was fairly small. Its whole purpose was to put a roof over her head and to store her food. This new structure had to be so much more. Draig decided he would build a *bereaern* (barley house), the word being pronounced 'barn'. Of course, Draig had no plans to store barley in it. This barn would not only make for a good place to house Onyxia but also the equipment required to make wine from the berry seeds he brought with him.

He thought about how to construct this barn. The barn would have a ground floor with crude stairs leading up to a loft above. He also decided he would need a large door in the front. As he sat there thinking about it, he glanced over to a bush and saw a spider building a web. Just then a small leaf floated onto the web. As he stared at the leaf that covered the spider web, Draig had an idea.

He picked up a piece of bark and drew a framework that somewhat resembled the framework of the spider's web. He reckoned that once the frame was completed, he would cut planks of wood to cover the frame much like the leaf covered the spider web.

Draig decided the best place for the stable was in the shade of the oak where the tree would protect it from the afternoon sun. He then figured that the house should face the oak tree. After all, the vision he saw of the dragon was under the oak tree, and therefore the house should face the vision.

Now, Draig had to decide what to build first. Logic told him that he should build the barn first. He reasoned that it would be an easy thing for Lucky and him to pull up a piece of the floor in the barn, but it would be a bit difficult for Onyxia to sleep in a house.

With everything decided, Draig gathered small sticks of about two feet in length. He used these sticks to mark the boundaries of the barn and the house. As it was a bit too late to start such a large project, Draig built a campfire to ward off any wild animals and settled in for the night.

The next day Draig was awakened by the warmth of the morning sun on his face. For the first time since he started this journey he had an uninterrupted night's sleep. With a full night's rest, he began to construct his barn.

Over the next few days Draig cut down small trees nearby to use them to construct the frame for his barn. Once he had a good supply of wood, he started building the frame in small sections since he had no one to assist him other than Onyxia and Lucky.

One day, while Draig was working on the frame, a Roman patrol happened by. They rode down to where Draig was working and the captain called down to Draig.

"By whose authority are you on this land?"

Draig snapped back, "By my own authority!"

"This land belongs to the Roman Empire! You have no authority to be on this land."

Draig smiled and answered, "The oak tree invited me to build here. I am here by its authority."

"What? Are you touched? Trees cannot talk!"

"Are you sure?" Draig asked, "Ever try to talk to one?"

"Of course not!" demanded the captain. "You cannot talk to trees!"

"I've talked to them on many occasions." Draig said. "Perhaps you should try sometime."

The captain demanded, "You are not authorized to be here. You will have to leave."

Draig walked over to the oak tree and reached down, pulling five gold coins from a sack tied to his saddle. He put the coins in the captain's palm, one coin at a time.

"Perhaps we can come to an arrangement that would allow my companions and I to stay here." Draig said.

The captain looked at the gold coins in his palm and then looked back to his men as if to ask their opinion. He then looked back at Draig. Obviously, this was not a significant enough of an enticement for the Romans.

Draig reached down and pulled five more gold coins from the sack and placed them in the captain's palm as he did with the others. The captain once again looked to his companions. They whispered among themselves and then all nodded to the captain. The captain quickly put the coins into his pocket.

"Thank you citizen, we hope you enjoy living here on your new farm."

The captain mounted his horse and the patrol rode away. Confident that he had come to satisfactory terms with the Romans, Draig returned to work on his barn. He labored on the frame for another week using a rope to raise one small section at a time. It was not an especially attractive frame, but function was more important than appearance.

It was the afternoon of the day that he finally completed the frame. He looked into his bags and realized he was running low on food. Onyxia could graze near the clearing for the time being, but Lucky and Draig were a different story. They needed meat, and meat did not just wander into camp and jump in the pot. It had to be hunted. With evening wearing on, Draig decided to hunt in the morning.

When morning came, he planned to hunt close to the clearing, so he had Onyxia and Lucky remain in camp. It would also make it easier to hunt without the heavy footsteps of a horse following behind him. Draig had spent the morning hours hunting down a few hares in the forest to the southwest of his farm. As he was walking home through some tall bushes, Draig heard a twig snap. It was not an 'animal in the forest' kind of twig snap. It was a human kind of a twig snap, but it was not a clumsy Roman soldier kind of a twig snap. It was more of a cautious, 'try- not-to-make-noise' kind of a twig snap.

As he came around the bushes and entered a small clearing, he suddenly came upon a party of warriors. Their faces were painted blue and were dressed in shirts and pants dyed brown. They carried crude but efficient swords. Draig knew they must be from the tribe native to the area but which he had not seen until now.

At first they were as surprised to see Draig as he was to see them, but the surprise was wearing off fast, and they were beginning to advance. Draig quickly dropped his bow and brought his palms together. He formed a ball of energy between his hands, and the ball became a fiery orb. He took the orb into his right hand and held it out in his open palm. Draig then blew on the orb, creating a large stream of flame that extended from the orb outward over the heads of the warriors. The flame was only meant as a warning.

The warriors dropped to their knees and trembled in fear. They hugged the ground with their faces buried in the dirt. They did not look upon Draig. Instead, they pleaded for their lives:

"Cinaed, Gahb troicare! Cinaed, GahbTroicare!"

Draig knew of Cinaed, though he had never met him. Cinaed was a dragon who lived in the northern part of the Great Plain near the cold Northern Sea. The people who lived there were called the Angeln, but surely these people could not be descendants of the Angeln.

The leader of this party of warriors finally got up the courage to speak, his voice cracking as he spoke:

"Cinaed, I . . . I beg you to . . . forgive us! We did not know it was you!"

So, these primitive people thought he was Cinaed. This was an interesting turn of events. While Draig did not like the idea of taking advantage of their superstitions, it was better than having to deal with them in a more finite way. If he had to be Cinaed, he would treat these people as Cinaed would have treated them. While still holding the fiery orb in his hand, he called out to them in the loudest voice he could muster.

"I am Cinaed! We are the Great Ones of your fathers!"

"Have mercy, Cinaed!" they cried as they cowered.

Draig shouted once again: "I have taken this new form. Look and remember for this is how you shall now know me in this place!"

The warriors slowly rose to their knees and trembled, hesitating to look up to set their eyes on Draig. A sense of utter fear filled their eyes. Slowly, the warriors began to back away, shielding their eyes from the one who they perceived was Cinaed, Master of Fire. Once they were what they considered a safe distance, they leapt to their feet and ran away as fast as their legs would take them.

With the warriors gone, Draig released the remaining energy that was the fiery orb. He then picked up his bow and continued his journey home. Now that the encounter was over, Draig had time to ponder what had occurred while he walked home.

The warriors thought he was Cinaed, the Great One and Master of Fire, who had brought the lessons of fire to many tribes in the north, but Draig had never interacted with tribes in Britannia. Therefore, these Angeln must have migrated here from that region of the great plain where Cinaed had influence. There could be no other explanation.

As always, whenever Draig reached home, Lucky and Onyxia were eagerly waiting for his return. They had both been standing beneath the great oak scanning the horizon for him. As soon as Lucky saw him, she ran to see what he had brought home for them to eat. Onyxia was simply glad he was home, and after acknowledging that she knew he was home, she wandered off to graze.

The next day Draig started collecting and splitting logs to make long, thin boards of varying sizes based on the girth of the log. While he remained preoccupied with his chore, Lucky came running up to him hissing and meowing. It was obvious that she was upset about something, so Draig turned and scanned the area where she was looking.

It did not take long for Draig to catch sight of several of the Angeln that he had encountered the day before. They were hiding in the trees just beyond the edge of the farm. This confirmed what he had feared when he first encountered them in the bush: they had found him and his farm.

Draig decided he should reinforce their lesson from the day before. He quickly brought his palms together. He formed a ball of energy between his hands. The ball of energy became a fiery orb. He took the orb into his right hand and tossed it down with a circular motion of his hand. A pillar of fire churned from the spot of the orb and rose into the air.

Startled by the spectacle of the swirling pillar of fire, the warriors turned and ran toward the south. With the warriors gone, Draig dissipated the pillar of fire and returned to his chores. He then caught sight of Lucky out of the corner of his eye as she held her head high and pranced around. He could tell that she was overly pleased with herself. He also wondered if this was normal behavior for a guardian cat!

The following morning Draig woke to find a large pile of boards stacked up neatly at the edge of the clearing. It was obvious that this was an offering from the Angeln. There were more than enough to complete both the barn and the house. It had to have taken the whole tribe all night long to cut all the boards.

Draig spent the whole morning moving the boards from the edge of the clearing to the barn. This gave him plenty of time to wonder just how long the Angeln had watched him before Lucky discovered their presence. It must have been a long time to give the Angeln enough time to figure out how Draig was making the boards and to duplicate the process.

As night came each day, Draig would sleep inside the unfinished barn with Onyxia and Lucky. Draig was once again returned to waking up every night because of his dreams, but they were not bothering him as much as before. It was simply becoming an irritation since he knew that these dreams must have meaning, even if he could not figure out what that could be. As all things come to an end, the barn was finally built.

With the barn completed, Draig built for himself a large wooden chest. He dragged it up the stairs and into the loft where he placed it against the wall. With Lucky watching attentively, Draig placed his armor and his sword into the chest, covered them with an old blanket and then closed the lid. Draig looked down at Lucky and smiled.

"Well, my littlest friend, the past is now safely put away."

Lucky purred in agreement. Draig went down the stairs and outside to pick through his pile of boards to find a suitable piece. From this piece of wood he made three wooden plaques and carved onto each plaque a different name—Bellorus, Dormanus and Melkoran. He then climbed back into the loft and hung the plaques on the wall behind the chest.

Draig knelt and bowed his head. "There you are, my friends," Draig said aloud, "so that I will never forget."

Draig rose and left the loft in silence with Lucky following close behind. Now that Onyxia's home was complete, it was time to begin working on the house. He framed the house to have two rooms, one for living and one for sleeping. He also built a fireplace for cooking and heating in the winter.

For two weeks, Draig spent his days building his house and his nights in the barn. Each night he would take a bottle of the wine out of his bag and walk up the stairs to the loft. He would pick up a cup that sat on the chest and fill the cup with wine, placing the bottle on the floor. Draig would then kneel on the floor and hold up his cup.

"Bellorus, old friend, I drink to your memory!" And he would take a sip from his cup.

"Dormanus, old friend, I drink to your memory!" And he would take a sip from his cup.

"Melkoran, old friend, I drink to your memory!" And he would take a sip from his cup.

Draig would finish the wine left in his cup and then put the cup back on top of the chest. He would pick up his bottle come down the stairs and put the bottle back in the sack. He would then go to sleep.

The day finally came for Draig to attach the last board to finish the house. He walked up to Onyxia and Lucky, who were standing between the house and the barn. He then addressed his friends:

"Well, my friends, what do the two of you think of the house I have built?"

Onyxia tapped the ground several times with her left hoof and let out a loud neigh. She then turned and walked into the barn. Lucky slowly walked up to the house and stuck her head in the door. After a moment of looking around, she walked inside and disappeared, leaving Draig standing outside all alone.

Draig threw up his arms. "Good, I am glad my house pleases you both."

Draig stood there as if something was supposed to happen, but nothing did. He looked around the edges of the clearing as if he hoped the Angeln were watching and would approve of his completed house. Finally, he shrugged, walked into the house and closed the door.

With the barn and house built, Draig's attention turned to starting his crops. He built a crude plow that Onyxia pulled to prepare the soil. After several days of plowing, Draig was ready to plant the seeds. The seeds would one day grow the most delicious berries, and those berries would one day become a most wonderful tasting wine.

At first, Lucky was so intrigued with every little detail that she followed Draig everywhere. Of course, it did not take long before Lucky came to the realization, in her tiny cat mind, that watching Draig do chores was almost as much work as doing chores herself. It was simple enough for her to reason that it was more fun to run and play than watch Draig do chores.

Onyxia was a different story. She was not all that interested in most of these activities. But when these chores involved plants, she was a little more attentive since they could easily translate into something edible. Onyxia spent far more time looking at the berry plants growing in the field and thinking they just might be a tasty treat.

From time to time Draig saw a Roman patrol pass by, though they never stopped to bother him. It was evident to Draig that the bribe he offered was sufficient payment so that no further contact was necessary. This pleased Draig as it left him time to perform his chores uninterrupted.

It was not long before his crop of berries was planted, leaving Draig time to find new projects to fill his time. He cleared away the weeds, trimmed overgrown plants and even planted a small garden. He even got around to building some crude stone benches and scattering them around the farm.

Lucky took a little more interest in this project. As Draig dragged these stone monsters around the farm, Lucky ran along in the furrows created by the weight of the large stones. Of course, even a cat's curiosity wanes after just a few benches. The last of the stone benches Draig set in the shade of the large oak tree.

It was soon the night of the full moon, and Draig was in the house eating his supper. Suddenly, Lucky began walking in circles and meowing loudly. The meows were long and drawn out, telling Draig that Lucky had heard something outside.

Draig grabbed a piece of firewood to use as a club and ran outside. Holding up the club, Draig scanned the farm. Suddenly he noticed two burning torches stuck in the ground at the edge of the farm. He saw two large baskets sitting between the torches.

Draig moved slowly toward the torches. He was looking around cautiously as he realized this could easily be a trap. Lucky followed a foot or so behind. It was obvious to Lucky that she did not feel this was a good time to be leading the way. As Draig neared the torches, he stopped and scanned the darkness for any sign of movement, but there was nothing but darkness.

Draig looked into the baskets to find fruits and berries. He also found meal bread and wild nuts. There were also two ducks that were freshly killed. It was obvious that it was meant as a tribute to Cinaed. It would bring dishonor to them if he did not accept the gift, so Draig took the gifts inside the house.

Over the following months Draig found little reason to leave the farm. Of course, sometimes it was absolutely necessary. He would leave the farm to collect wild oats for Onyxia. On these occasions, Draig brought Onyxia with him since there had to be someone along who was strong enough to carry a sufficient supply of wild oats to make the trip worthwhile.

Draig would also leave the farm to hunt for fresh meat for Lucky and himself. On these occasions, Onyxia generally chose to remain behind. Lucky would generally go along, though she would sometimes stay behind to keep Onyxia from being alone. On those hunting trips when Lucky accompanied him, she would track behind

Draig. She was obviously of the mind that she was helping hunt for the prey, and sometimes the prey Lucky found was not the same prey as Draig was hunting.

It was not always work around the farm. Sometimes fun invented itself. One day as Lucky sat in the open window of the house, Onyxia walked up close to the window. Lucky rose up and down as she eyed the situation. One could almost see the tiny gears turning in Lucky's mind. It was a simple feat for Lucky as she jumped from the window onto Onyxia's back.

Any other horse might have been spooked with having a cat leap onto their back, but Onyxia and Lucky were family, and so she simply turned her head to look as Lucky took her position at the front of her back and then started walking about the farm.

This became a pastime. Lucky would jump on and they would wander around the farm for hours. It was an easy matter for Onyxia to find a window sill, a pile of barrels, or anything else tall enough for Lucky to jump onto whenever it was time for Lucky to get down.

One day, while Draig tended to his chores, a Roman soldier happened by. He had been one of the soldiers to whom Draig had given the gold coins. The soldier approached Draig with a question that had been bothering him.

"Sir, I have ridden past your farm on a number of occasions and I simply had to stop and ask. Your wildcat rides your horse?"

Without skipping a beat, Draig replied, "Well, they tried it the other way around, but it did not work so well for the cat."

The soldier laughed and then followed up with another question. "No, I meant that it seems so unusual to me."

"Onyxia and Lucky have been friends for a very long time," Draig explained. "Being together is as natural to them as swimming is to a fish. They would not know how to act in any other way than how they do."

And then the soldier asked, "Sir, your animals are loose to roam wherever they wish? How do you keep them from leaving?"

Draig answered, "I don't. They are not just my friends. They are my family and this farm is their home. They have the right to go where they wish, but they do not leave because they choose to stay. When Onyxia gets tired, she goes to the barn and sleeps. When Lucky gets tired, she usually goes in the house and finds a nice place to lie down. I do as I please and they do as they please. This is what family does."

The Roman soldier was still a little stunned by the whole experience. If the Roman had known just how long that horse and that wildcat had been friends, he probably would have understood their deep connection to each other. The soldier finally rode away. He shared the story with his fellow soldiers so that whenever Roman soldiers passed the farm they would stop in the hopes they could see the wildcat riding the horse.

Over the next months, Draig focused almost exclusively on growing his crops. Every full moon the Angeln returned with their offerings of the two baskets of food. While Draig did not like taking these offerings from them under false pretenses, it was better than having to use force to control them.

The time finally came for Draig to harvest his berries. He used a bucket to put the berries in as he picked them. He then poured the berries into a large tub and repeated the process all day. It was a very slow process.

After spending the entire day picking berries, Draig was more than happy when it was time to go to bed. He wondered how many days it would take to harvest his entire crop. He estimated that it would take him about a fortnight to finish harvesting. He went to sleep hoping that his berries would not rot on the vine before he could finish picking them.

He woke up the next morning and went out to the barn to get his bucket. He stood in the doorway and could not believe what he saw. There were dozens of large baskets all filled with his berries. He ran out to the fields to find that every berry had been picked.

He returned to the barn and stood looking at all the berries. There was only one explanation. The Angeln had to have seen him harvesting his berries, and while he slept they harvested the rest of his crop. The whole tribe had to have come to complete the chore in just one night.

With the berries harvested, it was now time to convert the berries into wine. Draig began filling a large tub halfway with berries. He then stomped them until they were totally crushed. In the beginning, Lucky looked into the tub as Draig stomped around. Stomping berries sounded like fun to her, and she tried to climb into the tub. Draig had to push her back and explain to her that he appreciated the offer, but that hair in wine would not be appreciated by those who would drink the finished product.

Once crushed, most of the berries were poured into kegs to ferment into wine. A couple of kegs were used to produce a much more potent beverage known as dragon juice. It would take months for the wine to ferment, so Draig had to find ways to entertain himself.

Draig hunted from time to time. Sometimes he would encounter a few of the Angeln, but they kept their distance. He also tried fishing, but fishing was not nearly as much fun as it was with his friend Draco. Draig even began to look forward to his full-moon offerings as something to occupy his mind.

Eventually, the wine was ready to sell. Draig made a makeshift cart with two wheels, a flat top and two wooden arms that reached from the cart and tied to either side of Onyxia's saddle. At this point he loaded the kegs of wine onto the cart and tied them down so they did not move and risk overturning the cart. Draig then took the kegs to the Roman hill fort of Cunetio, which was merely a few bends in the river away.

Upon arriving, Draig offered free drinks to the garrison so as to secure their desire to purchase the rest of his product. He only gained a handful of silver coins for all of his labor, but it was his first season. His plants would produce more berries the next year, and he would already have a customer lined up and waiting to buy. He used the coins to purchase goods he could not obtain on his own and made his return home.

Chapter 2

The Farmer Takes a Wife

The next year passed slowly and without much incident. The Angeln continued to leave their full-moon offerings. The Roman patrols continued to stop to watch from a respectful distance Lucky ride around the farm on Onyxia's back. Draig and Lucky would occasionally go hunting while Onyxia usually remained behind to hold down the fort. And just once in a while, Draig would spot a few Angeln watching him from the safety of the trees.

His troubling dreams recurred during this time, and he still woke up in a cold sweat. The dreams, however, now took on a whole new dimension. He found himself in a thick fog and unable to see, but he was hearing but one voice speaking form beyond the fog. He could not only hear the words, but he could understand them. The words were familiar to him as he had heard them many times before. They were the words his teachers repeated to him often during the early years of his life.

"Take no action whose intent brings harm to another."

"The treoir is an energy that surrounds all things. It has been around since the begin time."

"There is no such thing as immortality, not even for dragons."

"Knowledge is a two-edged sword. Knowledge can be a great tool, but in the wrong hands it can bring with it horrific results."

"The more civilized Man becomes, the more violent he becomes."

Nearly every night it was the same dream, but with different words. As the months passed, he became accustomed to both the voices in his dreams and his new life as a farmer. He had to admit that life as a farmer was less exciting than his old life, but at least he had Lucky and Onyxia to keep him company.

When the second harvest season finally arrived, Draig took his bucket out to the field and collected berries until late in the afternoon. He put his bucket away in the barn and Lucky followed him into the house. Draig sat quietly while eating his supper and when he finished, he decided to retire early so that he would be well rested in the morning.

When Draig woke, he went to the barn to get his bucket. As he opened the door, he found baskets of berries stacked neatly on the floor. The Angeln had harvested the rest of the berries during the night, just as they had done the season before.

As he stood there staring at the baskets full of berries, he came to realize that the Angeln were watching their god more closely than he had originally thought. He felt guilt that he was benefitting from their misconception, and he also wondered how long they would continue to harvest his crops before they grew wary of the task. On the other hand, the Angeln had not grown wary of their regular full-moon ritual.

Draig spent the next few days crushing the berries and mixing them with herbs and spices in order to produce the desired wine. He then poured the berries into kegs to begin the fermenting process. With the kegs filled, he saddled Onyxia, grabbed a few gold coins from his coin sack and rode to Cunetio. Lucky chose to remain at the farm where she could bask lazily in the sunlight.

Draig had gone to Cunetio to locate a small wagon for transporting his wine. It had to be small enough for Onyxia to handle all by herself. Luckily for Draig, Cunetio was large enough to have a praefectus fabrum, under whom many artisans were employed, including a wagon-maker.

The praefectus fabrum was happy to direct Draig to the wagon-maker. Draig held out his hand to the wagon-maker so he could see the gold coins he held in his palm.

"Would you have a wagon I could buy for these few coins?"

"What size wagon do you need?" the wagon-maker asked.

"It needs to be large enough to haul my wine," Draig said, "but small enough that my horse can pull it all by herself."

"I'm afraid I do not," said the wagon-maker with a smile, "but I can build you one for those coins. After all, the wagon would bring us wine and we all love your wine."

"Thank you, sir. How long will it take to build so that I can come pick it up?"

"That will not be necessary, my friend, since our patrols pass your farm on a regular basis. It would be a simple task for a patrol to take it with them and deliver it to your farm."

"Thank you for your kindness, my good man."

Draig handed the wagon-maker the coins and rode home to wait for the wagon. He did not have to wait long when early one morning a patrol came by with the wagon. While the patrols generally sat at a distance, on this occasion the whole patrol rode down to the farm.

The patrol did not just come to deliver the wagon. They all wanted to see Lucky riding Onyxia up close. They also were hoping that Draig had a keg of wine that he would be willing to let them sample.

"Please, sire, might we see the wildcat riding the horse?" asked the captain.

Draig smiled and whistled loudly. Onyxia and Lucky both came running to see what Draig wanted. As they ran up, Draig leaned down to Lucky and spoke in a voice loud enough for the soldiers to hear.

"These soldiers would like to see you riding Onyxia. Are you willing to do that for them?"

Lucky turned and ran into the house as Onyxia walked over to the window. The patrol was taken by surprise as Lucky jumped out of the window and onto Onyxia's back. Onyxia pranced around the farm to the cheers of the Romans. Lucky held her head high as she sat at the front of Onyxia's back just below her neck. The more the Romans cheered, the more uppity the pair became. Draig could not help but laugh at the spectacle Onyxia and Lucky were making of themselves.

The Romans pulled coins from their pockets and begged to buy wine. How could Draig refuse such a simple request? And so the soldiers drank their wine while petting Onyxia and Lucky. The pair quite naturally soaked up all the attention. When the patrol finally left, they were all in very good spirits in more ways than one.

As the months passed, the wine matured. Draig went into the barn and harnessed Onyxia to the wagon. He pulled four kegs, one at a time, and loaded them onto the wagon. Draig lifted Lucky onto the wagon, and they rode north toward Cunetio with Lucky sitting next to Draig on the seat.

After a short ride, the wagon rolled to a stop inside the hill fort of Cunetio. As soon as the wagon came to a stop, Lucky jumped onto Onyxia's back and sat down. She held her head high in the hopes of a little attention, and she easily received it from the garrison. Draig quickly sold his wine for a handful of coins and used them to buy items he could not easily make on the farm.

Among other things, Draig bought Onyxia enough hay to fill the wagon. He also purchased a new blanket and some dried foods to supplement his diet that his little garden could not supply. The commander of Cunetio approached as Draig climbed into the seat of his wagon.

"My friend, the hill forts of Verlucio and Sorviodunum have heard of your wine. They have begged me to ask if you could sell them wine as well."

"My harvest was large this year, so I have enough to sell to them as well. I will go there after I unload my hay."

Draig waved to the garrison as he rode away. He got home as quickly as he could and was backing the wagon into the barn when two Roman soldiers came riding up. They jumped down from their horses and helped Draig unload the hay into the far corner of the barn and then helped load eight kegs of wine into the wagon. The soldiers then rode off as Draig headed his wagon toward the hill forts of Verlucio and Sorviodunum.

As Draig rode toward Verlucio, he thought about those soldiers showing up to help him. He naturally assumed that if they saw his wagon broken down on the road, they might stop and help, but he could only assume they helped him so that he would be able to get to the other hill forts quicker.

He delivered three kegs to Verlucio and three more to Sorviodunum. Just as he did in Cunetio, Draig used the coins he earned to buy clothing and supplies that he could not produce himself. Having two kegs left, Draig decided to ride farther south and try to sell them to the village of Sarum.

As Draig arrived at Sarum, the first thing he noticed was a woman at the edge of town. She was tall, thin, and had long brown hair with beautiful green eyes. Draig thought she was rather attractive considering the fact that she was chained to a tree.

As he rode through town, Draig wondered why a woman would be chained to a tree. He stopped at the tavern and carried one of his kegs of wine into the tavern and asked for the tavern keeper. After a free sample taste of Draig's wine, the tavern keeper was more than willing to buy the two kegs for a small number of coins. Draig then went out to the wagon and brought in the second keg.

As Draig was leaving Sarum, he saw two young boys throwing pieces of fruit and bread at the woman chained to the tree. Being as curious as anyone else, he stopped to watch for a moment. After all, the whole idea of a woman chained to a tree rather intrigued him. Suddenly a tall, thin man came running up.

The man yelled, "I said you were to feed her, not torment her! Get home so your mothers can punish you!"

As the two boys ran off, Draig asked the man, "Why do you have her chained to a tree?"

The man turned slowly to Draig and replied, "She is chained to the tree because she is a witch."

Draig looked at the woman chained to the tree. He then looked at the man. He again looked at the woman chained to the tree. Draig slowly climbed down from the wagon and walked over to the woman.

He then turned to the man and said, "Really? She is a witch? Are you certain?"

The man answered, "She touched a farmer's mule and the next day he died."

Draig asked, "The farmer died?"

For a moment, the man got a confused look on his face, "No, the mule died."

While Draig was not all that familiar with witches, he reasoned that if she were really a witch, she would have no trouble burning down the whole village, chain or no chain. Draig scratched his head and peered at the woman.

Being that Draig could not resist a good joke, he began to inspect the woman as if he were inspecting a horse. Draig scratched his head and began to inspect the woman as if he were buying a horse. He turned her head from side to side. He turned her around several times. He checked her legs to make sure she had not gone lame. He even reached into her mouth and checked her teeth. Draig was proud of himself for being able to keep a straight face while continuing to examine the woman.

Then Draig spoke to the man. "She is a witch, is she? Hmm … she does not look like a witch, but I have never seen a witch, so I will have to take your word for it. What are you planning to do with her?"

"We haven't decided yet, but it will probably involve a fire," the man said.

Draig looked at the woman and then back to the man. "I do not know about that. If she could kill a mule simply by touching it, imagine what she could do if you brought fire close enough for her to touch it."

Draig then reached into his pocket and pulled out two gold coins and held them out to the man. "I have always wanted a witch. I will buy her and rid you of the chore of dealing with her."

The man looked at the gold coins and then looked toward the center of town. It was obvious to Draig that the man was considering the offer. Draig pulled out two more coins and held out the four coins to the man. Once more the man looked at the gold coins and then looked toward the center of town.

Without speaking a word, the man took the four gold coins from Draig. He unchained the woman and tied her to a rope. He then tied the end of the rope to the back of Draig's wagon and walked away. Draig then climbed back into the wagon and rode away slowly with the woman in tow.

Draig rode slowly so that the woman could easily keep up. After all, he did not want her to lose her footing and end up dragging her on the ground. Once Draig saw that he was out of sight of the town, he stopped and took a long look back to make sure no one was watching. Draig pulled a hunting knife he had concealed under the seat, and then he dismounted.

"We are out of sight of the town," he said to the woman. "There is no more need for this rope."

Draig cut the rope from her wrists and helped the woman into the seat of the wagon. As he climbed into the seat beside her, he offered her some friendly advice.

"Sit still, woman. Lucky does not like being crowded, and she does not like sudden moves."

The woman looked down at Lucky and Lucky looked back at her. The woman cautiously moved far to the edge of the seat. It was true that Lucky was small, but the woman had no idea just how sharp the wildcat's claws might be.

Draig was quiet as they followed the road north. On the way the woman began to wonder what was to become of her. She was also curious why Draig would pay four gold coins to buy her freedom. The more time that passed, the more curious she became. Finally, she got up the courage to ask.

"Where are we going?"

"Home."

"Where is home?"

"North."

"How far north?" she asked.

Draig looked at her and then looked back at the road. Draig did not answer and so she did not press him further. The woman realized that she was not going to get anywhere with her questions, so she decided she would have to wait to find out where they were going.

As their journey continued, Lucky began taking more notice of their passenger. She was almost as curious about the woman as the woman was about her. The woman timidly reached out and placed her hand on Lucky and was surprised when Lucky purred. Draig smiled as he watched out of the corner of his eye.

It was not long before they arrived at the farm. Stopping in front of the barn, Draig helped the woman down. He then removed Onyxia's harness and pushed the wagon into the corner of the barn. His attention then turned to the woman.

"Woman, come here!"

The woman kept her head down, looking at the ground as she walked over to where Draig was standing.

"Do you see those stairs?" Draig asked.

She turned and looked at the stairs. "Yes, sire."

"The stairs and the loft above are forbidden," Draig demanded. "You may never go there under any circumstances. Do you understand my words?"

Without looking up she answered, "Yes, sire."

Draig took the woman by the arm and led her into the house as Lucky followed close behind.

"Okay, witch, you will cook and clean until you have earned the price I paid for you."

"And how long will that take?"

"That depends on you, witch."

"And then what will become of me?"

"Then you can leave. Or not leave. The choice is yours. You may make a bed wherever you like."

With that said Draig walked out and began his chores. At first, the woman stood in the doorway and watched him. She thought about the way he talked and the manner in which he carried himself. Draig reminded her more of a noble than a farmer. While this piqued her curiosity, she finally turned her attention back to the house.

As she looked around, it became obvious to her that Draig's housekeeping skills left much to be desired. As there was plenty of work to keep her busy, she went about her duties.

When supper time approached, Draig made his way back to the house. Upon entering, he quickly noted that the house was a great deal cleaner than it was when he left. He sat down at the table where a plate of meat and vegetables was already waiting for him.

"By the way, my name is Wilona. My father was a Roman officer and he brought my mother here with him. Since I was born here, when they returned to Rome I remained."

Without looking up from his plate, Draig said, "Greetings, Wilona, I am Draig, Drag . . . I am Draig."

Wilona asked, "I know you are not from this island and you are not a Roman. May I ask where you come from?"

"No, you may not!" Draig demanded.

"Why not?" Wilona asked.

"I had no past before I arrived here. It is forbidden for you to ask about it. You may only ask of what is, not of what was. Do you understand?"

"Yes, Draig."

Draig finished his supper and picked up a small bottle of wine from the shelf. He then made his way out the door. Wilona watched as he walked to the barn and disappeared inside. She then went to work on some old, worn out blankets that she wished to turn into curtains.

As Draig climbed the stairs into the loft, he picked up the cup that sat on the chest. As he did every night, Draig filled the cup with wine and placed the bottle on the floor. He knelt on the floor and held up the cup.

"Bellorus, old friend, I drink to your memory!" And he took a sip from his cup.

"Dormanus, old friend, I drink to your memory!" And he took a sip from his cup.

"Melkoran, old friend, I drink to your memory!" And he took a sip from his cup.

Draig then sat down on the floor and refilled his cup. He pushed the cork back into the bottle and sat silently sipping his wine. As he relived past memories, he began to weep, not because they were sad memories, but because there was no longer anyone with whom to share them. As he neared the bottom of the cup, he stood up.

"I drink to my oldest, dearest friend. I drink to your memory, Draco."

With that, he drank the last of the wine in his cup. He placed the cup back on top of the chest and picked up his bottle. Slowly, he made his way back to the house. Draig placed the bottle back on the shelf and then sat in his chair.

Wilona finished the last curtain and hung it up over the window. She then looked at Draig, who was sitting silently in his chair. He was simply staring off into the distance.

"Are you all right?" she asked.

Wiping a lone tear from his face, he replied, "I am fine. I am always fine."

Wilona asked, "Why do you go to the barn to drink?"

"I do not go to the barn to drink," Draig said. "I simply drink in the barn."

Wilona asked, "But why?"

"It is a debt I owe," Draig said. "You are forbidden to ask. It is that simple."

After a time, Draig fell asleep sitting in his chair, leaving Wilona awake by herself. As she sat there, her attention turned to the bed in the other room. She looked at the bed, and then she looked at Draig peacefully sleeping in the chair. Wilona, having realized that a perfectly good bed was going to waste, decided to make use of it. Climbing into the bed, she found it to be a bit hard for her liking, though it was better than sleeping on the floor. She soon joined Draig in blissful sleep.

Wilona was awakened in the middle of the night by talking from the other room. The voice was that of Draig. Since she could not imagine who he could be talking to at this late hour, she decided to investigate.

As she stood in the doorway to the main room, all she saw was Draig sleeping in his chair. Thinking it was simply her imagination, Wilona turned to go back to bed. Just then Draig spoke again.

"Where are you, my friend?"

After a short pause, he spoke again. "What do you mean, 'you are in my mind'? I do not understand. How can you be in my mind?"

After another short pause he said, "I hear your words, but I do not understand them. We once stood on the field of battle and struck fear in the hearts of mighty warriors. Now, I am but a farmer who battles nothing but the soil beneath my crops and the dreams that invade my sleep. I do not understand why I am here."

One more pause and he asked, "Why did you summon me to this place?"

After a long moment of silence, Wilona thought Draig was finished and turned again to return to bed. Suddenly, Draig spoke once more:

"What do you mean, an evil still breathes?"

When Draig slipped back into a more quiet sleep pattern, Wilona returned to the bed. She lay there thinking about what she had just witnessed and realized that Draig was not simply talking in his sleep. He was literally talking to someone in his sleep. She realized she was hearing only one side of a conversation. And what was the evil he spoke about?

She could not understand what he thought was so wrong about being a farmer, but at least in his dreams he appeared to think farming was beneath him. She was also beginning to realize that there was more to this man who slept in the chair than she had originally thought. And with that she started to drift off to sleep.

Over the next few days, Wilona spent more and more time watching Draig. She watched as he labored over his berries. She watched as he worked in the garden. She even watched as he sat on the stone bench beneath the oak tree to rest.

She enjoyed watching Draig interact with Lucky and Onyxia. She would watch them follow Draig around the farm as he talked to them. She found humor not only in the way he talked to them but that he talked with them. These were conversations, even though neither Lucky nor Onyxia could talk. It was almost as if he could read their minds through their body language.

Every night she watched Draig take his bottle of wine to the barn and return to the house after but a short time. Each time he returned, the bottle would have two cups less wine. Though she was curious why he went to the barn to drink, she was not to ask and so she did not.

It was not long before Wilona experienced her first full moon on the farm. She heard a noise outside and decided to go to the door to investigate. Just as she was about to open the door and look out, Draig put his hand upon her shoulder.

"Stay in the house. It will be safer if you remain inside."

Draig stepped outside and closed the door behind him. Wilona cracked the door open and looked out. As she watched Draig walk toward the edge of the farm she spotted two torches. Between the torches were two baskets. She watched as Draig scanned the darkness for a few moments. Finally, he leaned down, picked up the baskets and brought them back into the house.

"Where did those come from?"

"Tonight is the night of the full moon."

"I do not understand."

"Every full moon I receive two baskets from the Angeln as an offering."

"Why do they bring you an offering?"

"Because they think I am Cinaed, their fire god."

"What? Why do they think you are their god?"

"When I met them, I let them live. Is that not a good enough reason?"

"That makes no sense!"

"Why does it have to make sense?"

Wilona tried to make sense of the whole thing, but she simply did not understand, and Draig was being less than forthright about answering her questions. She could not grasp why they would think Draig was a god, and it was evident that Draig was not going to be of any help. She finally decided it was a waste of time to press further, and so she went to sleep.

Days turned into weeks and weeks turned into months. One night, as Draig knelt in the loft and honored his friends, he heard a voice from behind him.

"What are you planning to do with the woman?"

Draig jumped up and turned around to see a dragon standing in the loft. It was there but it was not there. Draig could see through to the wall behind him.

"What are you planning to do with the woman?" the dragon spirit asked again.

Draig stepped back until he fell against the chest. He was stunned and bewildered.

"Draco, is that you?" Draig asked.

The dragon spirit spoke once more, but his voice was much harsher than before. Obviously, he was quickly losing his patience.

"What are you planning to do with the woman?"

"Do you speak of the woman—Wilona? I had not thought about it. I do not know," Draig explained.

"She did not ask you to buy her freedom. You chose to offer it as a gift of kindness. How long does it take to repay a kindness?"

"I did not think about her leaving. I suppose I simply became accustomed to her presence."

"It is time for you to remove the chains of debt and set her free."

"I will tell her that she can leave, but what if she decides not to leave?"

"Then you must be joined to her as man and woman. There is a ritual that must be performed at the circle of stones. I will teach you the ritual."

The spirit of Draco explained to him the ritual and then vanished as quickly as it appeared. Draig picked up his bottle and returned to the house. As he sat in his chair, he watched Wilona working on her needlepoint. When she looked up from her project, Draig spoke:

"Your debt to me is repaid. You are now free to go."

"Where would I go?"

"You are free to go wherever you choose."

"But I have nowhere to go."

"Leave or stay. It makes no difference to me. This is not a prison. You may do as you wish."

"And if I choose to stay?" she asked.

"Then we would be joined one to another," Draig replied.

"Why?" Wilona asked.

"Because it is the right thing to do, and it is the honorable thing to do."

Wilona stood and put her hands on her hips. "Is that the only reason?"

Draig rose and stood there looking at Wilona. At first he simply stared one of those casual stares, and then an odd, puzzled look came across his face. After a few moments, he turned toward the bedroom and shrugged his shoulders.

"I suppose I have feelings," Draig confessed.

He then disappeared into the room and a smile came to Wilona's face. He did not say how or what he felt, but she knew he had feelings, so he did not have to say it. She knew Draig loved her in his own way and that was good enough for her. She figured that since Draig was a great winemaker, then she would be the wife of a great winemaker. She was happy as she lay down and went to sleep.

Early the next morning Draig woke and walked into the living room where Wilona lay sleeping. He gently nudged her.

"Wilona, wake up and put on the white dress that you made."

As Wilona began to stir, Draig walked out the door and walked into the barn with Lucky following close behind. He climbed the stairs into the loft, and to his surprise there was a finely crafted staff leaning against the chest.

Draig picked up the staff and held it in his hands. The top of the staff had seven consequent rings. Draig knew these to be the seven known elements. Below the rings were a circle of symbols. Some Draig did not know, but some he was familiar with such as the triquetra or infinite loop. In the center, where one would grip the staff, there was an interlaced knot design. It was not simply decorative; it would also help in obtaining a good grip on the staff without one's hands slipping. The bottom of the staff had a silver cap to protect the wood of the staff.

Draig looked around the loft for evidence of who had left the staff, but there was nothing out of order. Draig leaned the staff against the wall and opened the chest. He removed a dark brown robe and put it on and tied it with a yellow rope. He then picked up the staff and descended the stairs.

He saddled Onyxia and slid the staff into the saddle so that it was concealed. He then walked Onyxia to the door of the house. After waiting a moment, he called to Wilona who was still in the house.

"Wilona, come here that we be joined."

Wilona came out wearing the white dress she had made. Draig lifted her onto the saddle and placed Lucky at the front of the saddle where she always rode. Draig then climbed up behind Wilona, and they all rode toward the circle of stones.

"Where are we going?" Wilona asked.

"To be joined," Draig answered.

"Where does that take place?"

"The circle of stones."

"What is the circle of stones?" Wilona asked.

"It was once a sacred place, and for a small few it still is."

"What will we find there?"

"Stones," was Draig's only answer.

Wilona reckoned that once again her curiosity would go unsatisfied, but she surmised it would not be long before she would find out about the sacred place. They rode silently the rest of the trip.

Once at the edge of the circle of stones, Draig climbed down and then helped Wilona to the ground.

Draig removed the finely crafted staff from Onyxia's saddle and moved to the center of the circle. He drew a pentagram on the ground and then stepped inside the circle as Wilona looked on.

Draig turned to the north. "Lugnasa, ruler of the northern dragons, I summon thee."

He then tapped his staff on the ground three times, and a glowing orb appeared at the north side of the circle of stones.

Draig turned to the east. "Beltaine, ruler of the eastern dragons, I summon thee."

He tapped his staff on the ground three times, and a glowing orb appeared at the east side of the circle of stones.

Draig turned to the south. "Imbolic, ruler of the southern dragons, I summon thee."

He tapped his staff on the ground three times, and a glowing orb appeared at the south side of the circle of stones.

Draig turned to the west. "Samhain, ruler of the western dragons, I summon thee."

He tapped his staff on the ground three times and a glowing orb appeared at the west side of the circle of stones. Draig knelt and laid the staff before him:

"Great Mother, Tiamat! I beg your presence from beyond this realm!"

Soon an orb appeared slightly above Draig's head that began to oscillate between white and red. It oscillated slowly at first, and then it oscillated faster and faster until it appeared as but a blur. Draig rose and reached out his hand to Wilona. He brought her into the pentagram, and they knelt, the two of them.

"Great Mother, Tiamat! I seek your blessings as I join with this daughter of Man."

Draig took Wilona's right hand in his left hand and wrapped a red ribbon about their wrists as he looked into her eyes. A swirling mist rose from the center of the circle of stones as a great host of shadowy orbs appeared and danced about. The great stones began to glow a ghostly blue, and as the ground rumbled the stones released lightning bolts into the morning sky.

"As this ribbon is tied to our wrists, so are our lives tied to one another. We are no longer two souls. We are now but one soul occupying two bodies. In the eyes of the Great Mother, Tiamat, you are now one with us."

Wilona thought she heard a female voice and Draig knew he did. It was a soft voice and yet it was a noble voice that seemed to come from everywhere at once.

"In the eyes of this Host, the son of Man and the daughter of Man are joined. Those who were two are now one. Blessings of the Light go with you until the end of your days."

One by one, the orbs slowly flickered and faded. As Wilona and Draig rose to their feet, Draig saw several figures running away out of the corner of his eye. Obviously this ritual was not as private as Draig thought it was.

As they rode home, Wilona was once again beginning to realize that her husband was more than he appeared to be. She had heard legends about such things as she just witnessed, but she had never before seen them firsthand.

"The stones . . . they glowed." Wilona queried.

"Yes, they did," Draig said.

"So, my husband, are you the god of those who leave the offerings?"

"No, my wife, I am not their god."

"Are you someone else's god?"

"No, I am not a god."

"But you made the ground rumble and lightning reached up into the sky! Only a god could do that!"

"It was not I who made those things happen."

"Then who did make those things happen?"

"The Great Ones of my ancestors."

"Who are those that you called to at the ritual?"

"The Great Ones of my ancestors."

"Then you are a holy man?"

"Perhaps you might say I used to be."

"What is the mark you put upon the ground?"

Draig drew a pentagram on Wilona's back with his finger, "It is a symbol of great power, a focal point for the channeling of great energy."

Wilona experienced things that she could not explain, and answers were not forthcoming. She thought becoming Draig's wife would change things, and he would be more open with her about his past. But she was quickly learning that even in marriage Draig was protective of his past and who he was before he became a farmer.

It was only a few days after Draig and Wilona were joined that the next full moon arrived. Draig went out and collected the Angeln offering baskets and brought them into the house. Draig began putting the contents away when he found something resting at the bottom of one of the baskets. It was a small wooden box.

Handing the box to Wilona, he said, "This is obviously for you, my wife."

"Oh, it is so beautiful!" Wilona cried out.

The box was hand carved and an intricate symbol was carved into the top. The symbol consisted of a hollow triangle with spirals coming off each angle, rotating in a counter-clockwise direction.

"What is this symbol on the top?" she asked while running her fingers over the symbol.

"It is the symbol known as the Triskele. It represents the three realms," Draig explained. "It is a symbol associated with Brigandu, a great healer and a teacher of the practice of midwifery. The Angeln hold her almost as dear as they do Cinaed."

"What are the three realms?" Wilona asked.

Draig explained: "The first realm is that realm which we live in, that is, the physical realm. The second realm is the spiritual realm, the realm of the Otherworld. The third realm is the realm of the mind, the psyche and the dream."

Wilona opened the box, and resting inside was an onyx figurine on a gold chain. She pulled it from the box and looked at it. The figurine depicted some marvelous winged creature. She looked to Draig for an explanation. Draig took the necklace from her hand and placed it around her neck.

Draig explained: "The Angeln have given you a most marvelous gift. The figurine represents their god, Cinaed, in his true form. It is made of onyx because it is a protection amulet. According to their beliefs, as long as you wear the amulet, you are protected by Cinaed, Master of fire."

As Wilona marveled at her new charm, Draig thought about it for another reason. He knew that the Angeln knew of Cinaed, but he was not aware that they had seen Cinaed in his true form. The figurine left no doubt in his mind that they had indeed seen him. Draig decided it was not necessary to explain to Wilona what Cinaed was since she did not ask.

As the days passed and the berries grew, Wilona watched Draig working in the fields. Since they were now joined, she thought she should know more about this man who is her husband. Finally one night, her curiosity got the better of her, and when Draig came in from the fields, she began to ask.

"My husband, why is it that you hide your past from me?"

"I am not hiding my past from you. I am protecting you from my past."

"I do not understand."

Draig walked out the door and headed for the barn, and Wilona followed him. As Draig reached the barn door, Wilona stopped in the middle between the house and the barn.

"I do not understand!"

Draig turned and looked at Wilona. Draig brought his palms together. He formed a ball of energy between his hands. The ball of energy became a fiery orb. He took the orb into his right hand and held it out in his open palm. Draig then blew on the orb, creating a large stream of flame that extended from the orb outward over Wilona's head. She quickly dropped to her knees to avoid the flame as Onyxia and Lucky quickly moved to a safe distance. Draig then dissipated the orb.

While Wilona was still on her knees, Draig turned to walk away and called back to her:

"Some things are simply best left alone."

Wilona sat there in the dirt and thought about what just happened. She had just witnessed her husband create fire from thin air and then command it to shoot out over the top of her head. She quickly realized that it was not necessarily healthy to press him too hard. After all, he had told her repeatedly that his past was not a subject for discussion, yet she pushed the issue.

She had been with Draig long enough to know that he would not harm her since he had always been gentle with her, but now she was beginning to understand why the Angeln believed that Draig was a god. In fact, after this latest event, she was starting to believe that perhaps the Angeln were not that far off the mark.

She resolved not to press him any further about his past. If this is merely a hint of the man before he became a farmer, she worried what greater truth must be buried deep beneath the surface. She rose and went into the house to wait for Draig to return.

After a time, Draig finally came through the door and sat at the table. His meal was sitting there waiting for him as always. He sat down without saying a word and began to eat. Wilona sat down at her plate and looked at Draig's face for a hint of his mood.

"My husband, I am sorry that I asked about your past. I know I am not supposed to ask."

"There is no need to apologize, Wilona, as I took no offense. You are born of Man, and so it is your nature to be curious. I simply showed you there are things in this world one should not be too curious about."

"I will not ask again, Draig. This promise I make to you."

"Do not make a promise that you know you cannot keep. I accept that you will try, and that is all that you can do."

She thought about what Draig had said. He talked about Man as if he was neither born of Man nor governed by the nature of Man. She did not forget this fact, but for this evening she managed to contain her curiosity.

As Wilona drifted off to sleep, her dreams were filled with that which happened at the circle of stones as well as what occurred that night. She also dreamed about the Angeln and what they must have experienced to bring them to believe that Draig was their god.

The days continued to pass and life went back to normal. And so the events of that night began to fade. As weeks came and went, the offerings continued each full moon, and the time to harvest grew near. Draig spent more and more time tending the berries, and Wilona spent her time working in the small garden next to the house.

When the day came to harvest his crops, Draig took his customary walk to the barn to get his bucket. As he walked to the fields he waved to Wilona, who was watching from the doorway of the house. It was only a few minutes before Wilona ran to the barn. She found herself a bucket and quickly joined Draig in the fields.

Draig entertained Wilona with stories. As the afternoon was drawing to a close, Draig told her the story of a man with the head of a bull. Wilona gave Draig such a look when he finished the story. Draig looked into Wilona's eyes. He just smiled and began walking to the barn to empty his bucket. Wilona followed after him.

Wilona demanded to know more about the bull. "Surely, there could be no such thing as a man with the head of a bull."

"Would I tell you there was such a thing if I had not seen him with my own eyes?"

Stunned, Wilona begged, "You have actually seen him?"

"Has your husband ever lied to you?"

"No, never have I heard you lie to me."

Draig's stories seemed unreal, and yet she could sense a tone in his voice that told her if the stories were not true that he at least thought they were. They put their buckets in the barn and walked toward the house. It was then that Wilona took Draig by the arm.

"How long will it take to harvest the berries?"

Draig smiled. "Less time than you would think."

Draig walked into the house and left Wilona standing there with a confused look on her face. After a moment, she walked in and made supper. They ate and went to bed early in preparation of a long day of work.

The next morning they rose and went out to the barn. As Draig pushed the door open, Wilona was surprised when she saw all the baskets filled with berries.

"Oh my goodness, how is this possible?"

"I told you it would take less time than you would think. When I begin to harvest the berries, the Angeln show up in the middle of the night and pick them all."

"What do we do now?"

"We turn the berries into wine. I guess now is a good time for you to learn the family business."

Draig poured a basket full of berries into a tub. He turned to Wilona, knelt down and removed her shoes. He washed her feet and then lifted her up and put her down in the tub.

"Walk around in the tub so that the berries get crushed."

As she walked around in the tub, Lucky came up and put her paws on the edge of the tub and looked in. She then looked up at Draig, who gave Lucky a stern look.

"How many times do I have to tell you? No hair in the wine."

Lucky looked back into the tub and then got down. Draig laughed as she walked away. He simply could not bring himself to get mad at her since she was only trying to help.

Draig watched as Wilona stomped around in the tub. After a time, he went and pulled another tub next to hers and poured a basket of berries into it. He then took her arm and assisted her from the first tub and into the second.

Draig transferred the berries from the tub into a bucket and then added herbs and spices. Next, he poured the contents of the bucket into one of his kegs. Once the tub was empty, Draig moved it back next to Wilona and refilled it with a basket of berries. This process continued until all the berries were crushed and poured into kegs.

In the last two kegs, Draig placed some special ingredients into them and placed them in the far corner of the barn. There was already another keg sitting in the corner that he moved to the front. As Wilona washed her feet and legs, her curiosity overtook her.

"Why do you separate those that way?"

"These kegs do not contain wine. They are a special drink that I produce for my own enjoyment."

"It's not wine? What is it?"

"It's a strong drink. It's called dragon juice."

"Why is it called that?"

"That is what they called it. That is what they have always called it—nothing more, nothing less."

"Who called it dragon juice?"

"The ones who taught me how to make it."

Wilona was not getting the answer she was looking for, but then this was as direct an answer as she ever got when she asked Draig about anything. Draig washed out the tubs and the buckets, leaving nothing else to do but go into the house.

Over the following months they did little else than work in the garden. Occasionally, Draig would take Wilona hunting with him and Lucky would naturally go along. He tried to teach her how to use his bow, but she was better at killing trees than killing supper. Lucky made little noises when Wilona missed her target. She was certain that was Lucky's way of laughing at her.

The day arrived when the wine was finally ready for sale. Draig pulled the wagon out of the barn, hooked the harness to Onyxia and loaded four kegs of wine. He then called out to Wilona, who was still in the house:

"Come on, woman, let's get moving. The sun will not stand still just for us."

The first one out of the house was Lucky, running out of the door as if a demon was on her tail. She jumped into his arms, and he set her on the seat of the wagon. Wilona came strolling out of the door shortly after. Draig helped her into the wagon and then climbed up himself.

Their destination was Draig's first customer—the northern hill fort of Cunetio. It was a beautiful ride in the morning sun and Wilona enjoyed it greatly. When they arrived, the soldiers made quite a fuss over Wilona. They had seen her on the farm as their patrols passed by, but this was the first time they met her up close.

Lucky jumped from the wagon and onto Onyxia's back. Draig could tell that Lucky was a bit put off that Wilona was getting more attention than she was, so he leaned into her and talked to her.

"Do not be hurt. This is Wilona's first time here. Let her have her moment in the sun."

Lucky looked at Draig and then she looked at Wilona. She then jumped back to the wagon and crawled into Wilona's lap. Lucky was not getting all the attention, yet any attention was better than getting none at all.

Draig collected a handsome pay, a pay that had been growing with each season. As a belated wedding gift, the soldiers gave Wilona some fresh wild flowers and a bottle of bath oils that had been left at the fort when a noble visited with his wife.

All the way home, Wilona chattered on about how wonderful were the gifts she had received. This was the first time in her whole life that so many people made such a fuss over her, and she was not going to let this experience fade away without a fight.

When they arrived, Draig loaded the rest of the kegs of wine into the wagon while Wilona went to put her bottle of bath oils in a safe place. As they prepared to leave, Draig noticed that Lucky was not in the wagon. She obviously was still upset that she was not the center of attention. Regardless, they then began their ride south to the hill forts of Verlucio and Sorviodunum and beyond to the town of Sarum without her.

As had occurred at Cunetio, the barracks at the other two hill forts treated Wilona with equal fawning. While she was extremely flattered by all of the attention, the excitement was beginning to fade by the time they reached the gates of Sorviodunum. When they finally arrived on the outskirts of Sarum, Wilona had Draig pull up.

"What if they recognize me?"

"If they do, they will wish they had not," Draig said.

Knowing what Draig was capable of doing, Wilona was satisfied that she had nothing to worry about, so they proceeded to ride into town. As Draig assumed, no one thought twice about Wilona. Draig sold his last kegs of wine to the tavern keeper and wandered over to the general store.

"Is there anything you need, my wife?" Draig asked.

"I could use some cloth to make some new clothes."

"Pick out whatever you like. Look around, and if you like it, it is yours."

Wilona picked out some nice cloth in various colors. She also bought some thread to match. For herself, she selected a nice brush for her hair and a new pair of shoes. She stopped and looked at a very fine gown that was displayed in the store, yet she knew it was way too expensive for her to ever own. Draig paid for the things that she had picked out and took them to the wagon. After Wilona walked out of the door, Draig pointed to the fine gown she had looked at so longingly.

"Where did you come by that dress?" Draig asked the clerk.

"It was purchased for a noble woman," the store clerk said, "but she never came to collect it, so here it sits."

Draig looked at the silver coins in his hand and then reached into his pocket and pulled out two gold coins.

"Will this cover the cost of the dress?"

While taking the coins, the store clerk said, "Normally, I would likely say no, but since it is obvious that few in this town could ever afford it, I'll accept what you offer."

Draig handed her one more gold coin. "It is a surprise for my wife. My wagon is just outside. While we continue to look around town, can you cover it and place it under the seat of the wagon?"

"Yes, sire, as you wish."

Draig walked out and directed Wilona away from the wagon so the merchant could place the dress under the seat. After touring the town a bit, they returned to the wagon and began the long ride home. It had been a long day for Wilona, but she was pleased with how the day had gone.

When they arrived home, Wilona went into the house with her new items while Draig removed the harness from Onyxia and put the wagon in the barn. He then hid the dress behind his back as he entered the house.

Wilona asked, "What have you got there?"

"Close your eyes. It is a surprise for being such a good wife."

Wilona closed her eyes and held out her arms to receive the gift that Draig was hiding behind his back. As Draig laid the dress in her waiting arms, she opened her eyes, and she was so thrilled at what she saw that she began to cry.

"Why do you cry, my wife? Have I done something wrong?"

Wilona smiled and said, "This is the most beautiful dress I have ever seen. I am crying because I am so happy with your wonderful gift."

With a confused look on his face, Draig said, "You cry because you are happy? If I live to be six thousand years old, I will never understand women!"

Draig grabbed his bottle of wine off the shelf and stomped off to the barn. While Draig did not understand her emotions, he could see that buying the dress for her was well worth the three gold coins he spent for it.

After his ritual in the loft, he returned to the house. As he walked in the door, the first thing he saw was Wilona standing there in the new dress. She was even more beautiful than normal. She was so happy to own such a beautiful dress that she could not contain herself.

She wore the dress for a while longer and then took it off and carefully put it away. Draig was once again confused. She loved the dress so much and yet she took it off.

Draig asked, "Why did you take it off?"

"It is too beautiful to wear," she replied.

"But I bought it for you to wear."

"It is a most beautiful dress, but I do not wish to get it dirty."

Draig looked up and whispered, "Draco, this is one you will have to explain to me someday."

Wilona made supper. They ate and then went to bed. Draig went straight to sleep, but Wilona lay there thinking about the new dress. It meant a great deal to her because the dress reminded her of Draig.

This was the gentle man that Wilona had come to know. The dress was not cheap and still he bought it for her. Even though she had nowhere to wear it, she was still glad to have it. It was not simply a dress but a symbol of their lives together.

Chapter 3

A Dragon is Born

In the fifth year of Draig's new life, it came to pass that Wilona was with child. Draig was finally going to be a father, something he had thought about over the many years of his life, but he thought it was something he was not meant to be.

Wilona insisted on continuing her chores. She reasoned that being with child was not an illness but a normal part of life. While she was careful not to work too hard, she was not about to let such a natural thing slow her down. Her logic, though, lasted for only the first few months and then quickly came to an end.

As the time drew closer, Draig began limiting what she was allowed to do. At first, he restricted her from any chores outside of the house, including the garden which she loved to work. Later he demanded she refrain from doing any household chores, and the last straw came when he forbid her to even cook the meals.

Wilona kept insisting she could fend for herself, but Draig would have nothing of it. Between his chores, Draig would run back to the house and check on Wilona. He would tend to her needs before going out to perform his next chore. When he was not doing a chore he was at her side.

One night, shortly after midnight, Draig was awakened by a pounding on the door. Draig opened the door to find an Angeln woman standing there. When she saw Draig in the doorway, she dropped to her knees.

"I beg your forgiveness, Great Cinaed, but Brigandu came to me in a dream. She told me to come to help Cinaed's woman with her child."

Draig knew that since Brigandu had sent the woman, she had to be a midwife. While it was not a surprise to Draig that Brigandu would know about Wilona's condition, he was very surprised that she would send this woman in the middle of the night. Just then, Wilona let out a scream from the other room.

"My husband, our child is coming!"

The woman looked toward the other room and then looked back at Draig. Draig was noticeably nervous. Having never witnessed a birth before, he had no idea what needed to be done. All that he knew for sure was that for the first time in his long life he was scared to death. Yet, Draig knew the midwife was there to help, and so he was very thankful she was.

"Go! Do what Brigandu has commanded of you."

The woman rose and quickly ran into the room. Draig's hands began to tremble and his mouth became dry. He brought towels and boiled water. He did not know why he was boiling water, but for some reason he felt it was required of him. If nothing else, it kept him busy for a short time.

As time passed, Draig became more anxious, and hearing Wilona scream every few minutes or so did not help to relax him.

Draig decided it would be better for his nerves if he waited outside. Lucky and Onyxia paced with him, walking in a small circle between the house and the barn and back. In truth, there was little else any of them could have done.

Draig heard a rustling now and then just beyond the clearing. Occasionally, he could also make out the flickering of a torch some distance away. With all the excitement, Draig had not considered whether the midwife had come through the forest alone or with protection. It appeared her companions were waiting for her in the trees just beyond the edge of the farm.

When he got tired of pacing, Draig opened the door and peeked in to find out if anything had changed. Wilona let out a scream every few minutes, and then there was a long silence before she screamed again. Having to hear this was even worse than pacing, so he closed the door.

Morning arrived and Draig watched the sun rise in the east while he continued to wait. A night without sleep was beginning to show on his face. All that waiting was wearing on Lucky and Onyxia as well, but they were not about to desert Draig in his time of need.

There came a time when Draig finally dropped to the ground and sat in the dirt. He was exhausted, hungry, and still had not heard a word from the midwife. He began taking a hand full of dirt in his right hand and slowly letting the dirt flow into the palm of his left hand. He did this over and over just to pass the time.

As mid-morning approached, the Angeln midwife stepped to the door with a smile on her tired face. She dropped to one knee and then called out to her god:

"Great Cinaed, on this day a son has been born unto you."

"How is my woman?"

"Cinaed's woman is resting, my lord."

Draig placed his hand on the woman's head as she remained kneeling in front of him. The woman brought her hands tight to her chest and raised her eyes without moving her head. Draig took his hand away, and then ran into the house with Lucky on his heels while Onyxia did her best to peek into the open door.

The woman reached up and put her own hand on her head where Draig had touched her. She could not believe that her god laid his hand upon her. This simple act by Draig would chase her life forever, and if her comrades witnessed it from the tree line, it would greatly raise her position within the village since no one else had ever been touched by Cinaed.

Draig entered the room to see Wilona lying on the bed with eyes closed and sweat still dripping from her face. He reached into a basin filled with water and pulled out a rag. He wrung it out and wiped her face with it.

He then took her hand and held it gently.

"How are you, my wife?"

In a soft voice Wilona said, "I am all right. I have heard our baby cry, but I have not seen it. What have I given my husband?"

"You have given me a son, my wife. Sleep now and let your strength return."

The midwife came in and sat on the floor next to the bed. Draig stood and watched Wilona as she rested. He then looked at the midwife and smiled. Draig went out to the other room and gently picked up his son. The boy had inherited many of his father's physical traits. Though he had little hair, it was blonde like his father, and his eyes were the same hazel-green.

Draig placed his son down and covered him with a blanket. He picked up his bottle and headed to the barn with Lucky in tow. After climbing the stairs into the loft, Draig picked up his cup and filled it with wine. He took a sip and sat in front of the chest as Lucky curled up on the floor nearby.

"My dear friends, today I drink with you, not only as a warrior but as a father. Wilona has given me a son."

As Draig sipped his wine, Lucky sat up and perked her ears. The loft slowly began to grow brighter, and suddenly there came a familiar voice from behind him.

"As I whispered to your mother so many years ago, I now come to whisper to you, Draig."

Draig jumped up and turned around to catch sight of a large dragon standing in the back of the loft. As before, he was there but he was not there as Draig could see through him to the wall behind. Draig gave out a great smile.

"Draco! I am a father!"

"So I have heard," the spirit of Draco said with a smile.

"Was it you who sent the midwife?"

"What would I know about human women giving birth? It was Brigandu who knew the child was coming and who spoke to the girl in her dreams. Besides, the girl would have been a bit confused hearing my voice speaking for Brigandu."

"I guess you are right, Draco. I had not thought of that."

"Now for the reason I have come, Draig. Your son must be given a name suitable of his heritage. Tonight you shall bring your son to the circle of stones. Just as I once whispered to your mother, I now whisper to you."

"Yes, Draco, as you wish."

With that said, the spirit of Draco vanished, the loft growing dim and Draig was left all alone. Draig finished his drink, picked up the bottle and returned to the house. As he reached the door, Lucky was waiting for him.

Draig asked, "What is wrong, Lucky, did you not recognize our friend?"

Lucky just sat there looking up at him, so he went into the house. He leaned over his son and gently placed his hand on his head. As his son lay sleeping Draig spoke to him in a gentle voice.

"I need to rest, my son, and then we shall take a trip. There are those who are waiting to meet you."

Draig sat in his chair and thought about this day and its meaning. With the birth of his son, Draig had once more become a part of the world of Man. Draig was at once happy and sad. Within a few minutes, he drifted off to sleep.

It was late afternoon when Draig woke up from his nap. He went in and checked on Wilona. She was still sleeping, and the midwife was sitting on the floor watching over her.

Draig leaned down to the midwife and whispered, "There is a task to which I must attend. I leave her in your hands until I return."

Draig walked out to the barn. He saddled Onyxia and walked her to the front of the house. Draig wrapped his son in a blanket, placed him in a basket and walked outside. He first lifted Lucky up onto the saddle, and then he held his son tight to his chest with one hand as he climbed into the saddle and rode to the circle of stones.

Darkness had fallen by the time they arrived. Draig climbed down from Onyxia and placed the basket at his side. Next, he brought his palms together and formed a ball of energy between his hands. The ball of energy became a fiery orb. Taking the orb into his right hand, he held it out in his open palm and let the orb grow bright. The orb rose into the air and hovered above the circle of stones as it lit the area in a faint light.

Draig pulled his staff from Onyxia's saddle and walked to the center of the circle. He drew a pentagram on the ground with the end of the staff. He then stood in the center of the pentagram and laid the basket that held his son on the ground in front of him.

Draig turned to the north. "Lugnasa, ruler of the northern dragons, I summon thee."

He then tapped his staff on the ground three times, and a glowing orb appeared at the north side of the circle of stones.

Draig turned to the east. "Beltaine, ruler of the eastern dragons, I summon thee."

He then tapped his staff on the ground three times, and a glowing orb appeared at the east side of the circle of stones.

Draig turned to the south. "Imbolic, ruler of the southern dragons, I summon thee."

He then tapped his staff on the ground three times, and a glowing orb appeared at the south side of the circle of stones.

Draig turned to the west. "Samhain, ruler of the western dragons, I summon thee."

He then tapped his staff on the ground three times, and a glowing orb appeared at the west side of the circle of stones.

Draig then raised his hands to the sky and called out:

"Draconos, I summon thee! Come into the light and honor me with your presence!"

After a moment, a ghostly orb formed at the edge of the circle and slowly approached. When it was but a few feet away from Draig, it came to a rest, floating a few feet above the ground. Slowly the orb took shape and became a dragon in spirit form. Then there came a voice that seemed to come from nowhere and yet everywhere.

"You have summoned me and I have come."

Draig took his son from the basket and held him out so that the spirit of Draco could see him. There was great pride in Draig's eyes as he held out his son.

"Look upon my son and give him your blessing!"

"On the day that we left, Tiamat deemed you a dragon for the sacrifices made by you and your comrades. That means your son is born of dragon. For that reason you shall name your son Drakeson, meaning 'son of dragon.'"

Soon, many ghostly orbs appeared and moved about. They moved in and out of the stones as if they were dancing. A single glowing orb descended from the sky and hovered above the circle of stones. Draig raised his son above his head as a voice came from the glowing orb.

"I, Tiamat, have come to honor thy son."

"As I am dragon, so shall my son be of dragon," Draig proclaimed. "Behold my son who shall be called Drakeson!"

Tiamat said, "Drakeson, son of Draig, son of Anarcher, son of Eafa, welcome to this world, son of dragon."

Draig lowered his son and held him to his chest. "Thank you, Great Mother. You honor me with your words."

"As I am your friend," the spirit of Draco said, "so it shall be with your son. I shall watch over Drakeson all the years of his life and beyond."

"Thank you, my dear friend," Draig said. "Thank you, all my friends!"

One after another, the ghostly orbs slowly faded away until but one remained. It continued to hover for a few moments and then finally disappeared. As Draig placed his son back into the basket, the spirit of Draco transformed into a ghostly orb once more. It hovered for a moment and then vanished. Draig stood there silently for a moment and then mounted Onyxia and rode home.

Wilona was sitting up waiting for Draig when he entered the house. The midwife knelt when she saw Draig enter. He laid Drakeson down and turned to the midwife. He placed three shiny gold coins in her hand.

"You have completed your duties. This is a reward for you. Brigandu is proud of what you have done."

"Thank you, my lord."

Clutching the coins tightly in her hand, the midwife rose to her feet and departed. It was then that Wilona questioned Draig.

"Where have you been, my husband?"

"I took our son to the circle of stones so that his birth could be blessed by the Great Ones of my ancestors."

"Why did you not wait until I was strong enough to go with you?"

"This day that our son was born is not an ordinary day. It is the most sacred day of the Great Ones. It is on this day that the doorway to the Otherworld opens and those who have died cross over. He had to be named while the two realms were connected before the magic was gone. Do you understand?"

"Yes and no, my husband," she said. "What name have you given to our son?"

"It was whispered to me that I call him Drakeson. He is Drakeson, son of Draig, son of Anarcher, son of Eafa."

Wilona thought about why Draig gave this particular name to their son. She knew that the name meant 'son of dragon,' but that did not make sense to her because her husband is not a dragon. He is a man. Though she was bewildered as to why Draig would name him so, there were many things he did that she did not understand. Draig was simply being Draig.

"Let me hold Drakeson," she said as she held out her arms.

Draig handed Wilona their son. As Wilona began nursing her son, Draig grabbed his wine and went out to the barn. This was one ritual he did not change, not even for the birth of his son. Wilona found this odd, but she found many things Draig did to be odd.

Wilona woke early the next morning to find that Draig was already up and about. He had been up since before sunrise. She heard a noise outside and went to investigate. She opened the door to see Draig laboring over small trees that he had fallen and dragged to the middle of the clearing.

"What are you doing, my husband?"

"Drakeson will need his own room, so I am doing something about it."

"But he will not need his own room for a long time."

"If I build it now, I will not have to build it later."

Wilona shook her head and walked back into the house. Draig spent all morning cutting the small logs into eight-foot lengths. This had reminded him of a chore he had once done with Draco many years ago. As noon approached he tended to his other chores so as to not get behind. When he finished his chores, he went in and ate his supper and then went out to the barn as usual.

This continued for several days until he had enough small logs to construct the walls of the new room. He took the next day off to rest. After all, chopping wood takes a lot of energy out of a man, especially if you do it several days in a row.

The next morning Wilona woke to a strange noise. It took her time to realize that it was the sound of someone walking on the roof. She quickly ran outside and saw Draig on the roof. He leaned the small logs against the side of the house so he could drag them up one at a time without having to climb up and down.

"Whatever are you doing up there?"

"I am building Drakeson's room."

"On the roof?"

"Yes, it seemed a good place. All I have to do when I am done is cut a hole and put up a ladder."

Wilona thought about it for a moment and decided to simply let it go since Draig was going to do it his way anyway. She went in the house and closed the door, leaving Draig to his project.

It was fairly easy to build the four walls. Draig notched each end of the logs so that they interlocked. He then combined pine pitch, beeswax and sawdust to make a resin for waterproofing and to prevent drafts between the logs. He also built in a window that faced the barn.

One day, Wilona heard a loud banging on the roof. She did her best to ignore the noise until there was a big bang. She turned around to see a large piece of the ceiling lying on the floor. She looked up and to her surprise there was Draig's head sticking through a hole in the roof.

"I promise I will clean that up."

"Are you done playing, my husband?"

"Yes, my wife, at least until I have eaten a midday meal."

"Is that supposed to be a hint, my husband?" Wilona asked with a smile.

"That is very possible, my wife."

There was nothing that Wilona could do but shake her head and get to work preparing them a midday meal. She had no idea why Draig was in such a hurry to build a room that their son could not use for years, but Draig was like that, so she simply had to deal with it.

After they shared their meal, Draig got up and headed for the door. Wilona looked at the mess on the floor and then looked at Draig. She called to him while the door was still open.

"What about this mess? You said you would clean it up."

"I will. . . I promised, did I not?" Drake answered.

Wilona was not as shocked as most wives would have been, but then most wives are not joined to someone like Draig. She calmly sat down and worked on her needlepoint and ignored the mess on the floor.

Draig spent the next several of hours putting the roof on Drakeson's new room. Soon after, Draig entered the house and cleaned up the mess he had left on the floor. With the mess cleaned up, he went out and brought in a ladder that he pushed into the hole in the ceiling and lashed the ladder down so it would not move. With his task completed he sat down in his chair and rested.

On the first full moon after Drakeson's birth, Draig went out to collect the offering from the Angeln. He brought the baskets in and began to rummage through them. At the bottom of one of the baskets were two objects wrapped in cloth. Draig removed the cloth from the first object to find a winged creature carved out of oak. It was the same winged creature as depicted on Wilona's onyx charm. Draig removed the cloth from the second object to find it resembled a red deer stag. Draig showed these to Wilona. She laid these two objects next to Drakeson. These gifts were Drakeson's first toys.

Time passed and Drakeson was soon old enough to crawl. Drakeson was constantly crawling after Lucky, who had become his favorite squeeze toy. She put up with this for only so long before she would find a place well out of his reach.

As soon as Drakeson was old enough to walk, he started following his father around the farm. He followed his father into the field as he tended to the berries. He followed his father while he tended the garden. He followed his father into the barn. Wherever Draig went, Drakeson was close behind.

One day Drakeson followed his father into the barn while he was doing his chores. When Draig moved oats to feed Onyxia, Drakeson grabbed a tiny handful of oats and brought them over for Onyxia. Draig laughed hysterically as Onyxia gently took the oats from his extended hand.

Drakeson then grabbed Onyxia's brush and was all smiles as he brushed her leg which was as high as he could reach. Draig lifted him up so he could brush Onyxia's side. He then put Drakeson down and took the brush to give Onyxia a proper brushing.

As he watched his father brushing Onyxia, his eyes became fixed on the stairs to the loft. Since he had never been in the loft, he was naturally curious what was up there. As he continued to stare at the stairs, his curiosity overcame him and he started to climb the stairs on all fours.

He felt a tug on his shirt as Draig grabbed a handful of cloth, pulling him off the stairs and into the air in one quick yank. As Draig put him down he yelled:

"No! Those stairs are forbidden! You may never go there! Do you understand me?"

Drakeson looked at his father and slowly took a step backwards. He looked at the stairs and then back at his father and began to cry. As tears ran down his face, Draig realized that he was a bit too stern with his young son. Draig knelt before him.

"I am sorry, my son. I did not mean to scare you. The loft and all that is up there is forbidden. It is not because I am mean. It is because I am protecting you from something that you are best not to know."

Within minutes, the tears dried up and Drakeson was once again running around and smiling as if nothing had happened. That does not mean that the lesson was not learned, but Draig took every opportunity to remind Drakeson that the stairs and the loft were definitely off limits.

As time passed, Drakeson continued to stick to his father like a shadow, watching his every move. As his vocabulary increased, he began asking questions. Actually, it was the same questions over and over.

"What you doing?" and "Why?"

As would any good father, Draig stopped what he was doing and patiently explained to his son exactly what he was doing and why he was doing it. Of course, Drakeson would be there the next time that Draig did the same thing, asking the same questions asked by small children with short memories. While it would often get on Draig's nerves to have to explain everything to Drakeson more than once, he also knew it was important to encourage a boy's desire to learn.

As Drakeson continued to grow, his vocabulary also grew. This brought Draig to take advantage of his shadow following him around for endless hours. He decided this presented an excellent opportunity to teach Drakeson what the son of a dragon needed to learn.

He put his hand on Drakeson's chest and said,

"You are Drakeson, son of Draig, son of Anarcher, son of Eafa. You are not just an individual. You are the product of those who came before you."

It was not enough to simply teach Drakeson the names of his ancestors. Draig would often repeat the stories he had learned from the storyteller when he himself was but a small child. He told of the great deeds of Anarcher and Eafa so that Drakeson would learn about those who contributed to whom he was. For Draig, this was a tradition of his forefathers and so it was a tradition for him.

Drakeson continued to follow his father and repeat what his father told him was his full name, doing so over and over:

"I am Drakeson, son of Draig, son of Anarcher, son of Eafa."

Drakeson did not just repeat his name; he also repeated the stories his father taught him. He repeated the story of Anarcher, the hero of 'an treas abhainn.' He recounted how Eafa slew a brown bear with nothing but the leg bone of a red deer.

Once Drakeson had learned this first lesson well, Draig moved on to the next lesson. Draig bent over and held up his index finger right in Drakeson's face.

Draig spoke firmly. "The first law: Take no action whose intent brings harm to others. One's actions are neither good nor evil, but rather the intent of such actions will determine whether it be good or evil."

Draig could see that this was a difficult subject for Drakeson's young mind to grasp. Draig then decided to explain the first law the same way it was explained to him many years ago.

"If you kill a man," Draig said, "one might say that the intent of the act is evil. Yet, does it not depend on what caused you to kill the man? If you kill the man for his possessions, then the intent is evil. You took an action whose intent brought harm to another. This is because the intent of the act was to take his possessions. The killing of him simply adds to the transgression. Now, if the man was chasing a small child with a blade, with the goal to harm the child, and you were forced to kill the man, the intent was not to bring harm to the man; the intent was to protect the child. Do you see the difference?"

"Yes, Father," Drakeson said.

It was not long before Drakeson was repeating the law right along with his father, but Draig was not so sure if his son truly understood. With Drakeson in tow, Draig repeated this law over and over as he went about his chores. As Draig continued to recite the law, he also continued to use examples which were easier to understand. Eventually, Drakeson learned not only the law but what the law meant.

"The first law, take no action whose intent brings harm to others."

Once Drakeson knew what this law meant, it was time to learn the next lesson. Drakeson was just as enthusiastic about this lesson as he was the last.

"The third law…" and Draig paused.

"Yes, Father?"

And then Draig yelled, "Protect the book!"

Drakeson's eyes opened wide as he took a step back. Draig began to smile and Drakeson laughed out loud. This law was a bit easier for him to learn. That night, while sitting at the supper table, the two of them had fun with it.

"The third law…" Drakeson said with a pause.

He looked at his father and his father looked back. They slowly moved their head closer together. When they were face to face, they both yelled together:

"Protect the book!"

They both laughed boisterously while Wilona had one of those 'boys will be boys' looks on her face. They did it several more times during the meal. Each time they did it, they laughed louder. Drakeson was definitely enjoying learning this particular law.

After supper, Draig picked up his bottle and went out to the barn, as was his normal routine. After he left, Drakeson decided to jump into his father's chair. At first he sat there with his arms crossed. He then placed them on the rests of the chair. Suddenly, without warning he said.

"The third law…" he said with a pause. He then yelled, "Protect the book!"

His mother looked up from her needlepoint and smiled. She was glad that he was so excited to learn from his father.

With his hands on the arms of the chair, he began to rock back and forth. After a few minutes he slumped back into the seat and sat quietly thinking. Suddenly, he sat up and turned to his mother.

"Mother, what book?"

Wilona simply smiled and answered, "You are asking the wrong person, dear."

"Why?"

"Only your father knows the answer."

With no answer to his question, Drakeson got up and played with the two wooden toys that the Angeln made for him. By the time Draig returned from the barn, Drakeson had lost interest in getting an explanation as to which book the third law applied, and so he went to bed. Wilona figured that was probably a good thing since Draig seemed so reluctant to explain certain things.

The next morning, Drakeson woke and came into the living room. He crawled into his father's lap and tugged on his shirt. He then asked the question that had gone unanswered from the night before.

"Father, we are to protect the book. What book?"

Draig explained: "The Book of Knowledge was created in the begin time. It is written in a long forgotten begin time language. It is constructed of etched golden plates and bound in leather. It is the accumulated knowledge of the Great Ones and beyond. This book must be protected, for while knowledge is a powerful tool, the Great Ones realized long ago that knowledge in the wrong hands can be terribly destructive. This is why we must protect the book even with our very lives."

"That is the book we protect, Father?"

"Yes, my son, that is the book." Draig answered.

"The Great Ones of my ancestors?"

"Yes, my son, the Great Ones of our ancestors."

"Have you ever seen the book? Drakeson asked.

"Yes, my son, I have laid my hands upon the book and read its words," Draig said with great pride.

"Tell me, Father! Tell me more about the book!"

"Far from here is a forbidden mountain," Draig began. "At the base of that mountain is the entrance to a great cavern. The opening is large enough for an oak tree to grow in its mouth. I followed a number of deep passages which continued on for what seemed like forever. I could sense that I was going deeper and deeper into the earth. As I continued to go deeper, it became obvious that these were not natural passages. These passages were cut from the solid rock that surrounded them.

At last I came to a great vaulted chamber filled with pillars of solid crystal. These crystals glowed and bathed the entire chamber in a soft light. In the center of the chamber a circular crystal rose up from the ground to form a table. As I drew near, I could see the book resting on top of the crystal. Across the front of the book were the words 'Leabhar Seo Eolas' embossed in large letters. It was the Book of Knowledge."

"You opened the book and read from it?" Drakeson asked.

"Yes, my son. Now, go and play. I will come out soon to do my chores."

Drakeson got up and ran outside. Wilona watched Draig for a few moments before walking up to Draig and putting her arms around him. After giving him a long hug, she gave him a kiss.

"What was that for?"

"You are such a good father to our son."

With that, Draig rose and went out to do his chores. Wilona did not know if the Book of Knowledge was real or a legend, but it did not matter because Drakeson believed it. Wilona saw that Drakeson was slowly becoming his father, a little bit each day.

The lessons continued, one after another, as the days became weeks and the weeks became months. Wilona would laugh whenever Drakeson started repeating something new he learned from his father. She thought it was so amusing to watch her son mimic the words of his father. As Drakeson got older, he not only began to look more and more like his father, he began to sound more like him.

During the early years of Drakeson's childhood, Draig was forced to harvest the berries alone. In the first couple of years Wilona had to remain inside to care of their son. As Drakeson grew older, Wilona watched him near the field so that she could help a bit while caring for him at the same time. The sixth harvest since Drakeson was born had arrived, but this year was different. Draig decided that Drakeson was finally old enough to help pick the berries. Draig went into the barn and gathered up buckets while Wilona took Drakeson out to the field.

Draig patiently showed Drakeson how to pick the berries and put them in the bucket. Draig and Wilona gathered berries and carried them to the barn all day, though Drakeson only lasted a couple hours before he got tired and fell asleep under the oak tree. Lucky saw that Drakeson had a really good idea and curled up next to him and went to sleep as well.

It was late afternoon when Drakeson rejoined his parents to pick more berries. At the rate he picked berries, Drakeson only filled one more bucket at quitting time, but Draig still thought the boy did his fair share. They put the buckets away and went into the house to eat their supper.

Drakeson was tired and barely picked at his food. Wilona had little trouble getting him to bed since he was falling asleep at the supper table anyway. Draig and Wilona also retired early since it tomorrow would be a long day for them.

They woke early in the morning and headed for the barn. As Draig pulled the barn door open, Drakeson saw the baskets of berries that the Angeln had harvested during the night, but Draig and Wilona were the shocked ones as Drakeson barely took notice.

Draig washed Wilona's feet and poured a basket of berries in a tub. He then picked her up and put her into the tub. As she stomped around in the tub, Drakeson came over to the tub and tried to climb in. Draig pulled him aside and washed his feet and then placed him in the tub with Wilona.

Wilona held Drakeson's hands as they pranced around in the tub. This was like dancing to Drakeson. For him, this was not work but a game that he had never played. Tub after tub, he laughed and danced. Of course, all good things come to an end and he wore out his little body.

Draig pulled Drakeson out of the tub and placed him where he could watch the rest of the process. While Wilona continued to crush the berries, Draig showed little Drakeson which herbs and spices to put in and in what quantities. He would then pour the mixture into kegs to ferment. He hoped that Drakeson would learn enough to make the wine easier the next year.

As the months passed, Draig returned to his chores and Drakeson went back to following his father around the farm, but it was the same thing every time Drakeson followed Draig into the barn:

"Is the wine ready yet?" Drakeson asked.

"No, it is not ready yet."

"When will it be ready?"

"Soon, my son, soon."

Fortunately for Draig's sanity, the day finally came that the wine was ready for sale. Draig hooked up the wagon to Onyxia and loaded six kegs of wine. When he was ready to leave for Cunetio, Draig called to his son.

"Drakeson, come here. It is time you learn about the selling part of how your father makes his living."

Drakeson ran out to him as Wilona stood in the doorway and watched. Draig lifted him onto the seat and put Lucky next to him. He then climbed up into the seat and called down to Wilona.

"Do you wish to come too, my wife?"

"No, this is a bonding thing for you and our son. I will stay home this trip and let the two of you share the experience."

"Is there anything you need from Cunetio?"

"Nothing special, my husband. When you return, I will have a meal ready for my two men."

Drakeson was excited to be going on a trip that would take him away from home for the first time. Until now, he had to stay home and simply watch his father ride away. As he rode to the hill fort with Lucky on his lap, every couple of minutes he asked the same question:

"Are we there yet?"

"Almost there."

"Are we there yet?"

"Almost there."

This exchange continued until Cunetio finally became visible in the distance. When they arrived in Cunetio, Lucky leaped from Drakeson's lap and onto Onyxia's back. She wanted to make sure she got as much attention as was possible. When Draig lifted Drakeson down from the wagon, his first impulse was to hold onto his father's pants and stay as close as possible. He never seemed to be shy in the past, but this was the first time he had been around so many strangers at one time.

As Drakeson became more comfortable around so many people, he let go of his father's pants and began to wander around, though he didn't wander too far from the wagon. He became especially intrigued when he saw some soldiers practicing nearby. This was the first time he saw people using swords, even if it was just practice.

Once Draig had sold his kegs of wine, he began to look for things to buy with the handful of coins he received. Draig began by filling the wagon with hay and necessities which he could not grow in their garden. Other things had to wait until he got to the storekeeper in Serum.

Draig's attention finally turned to his son, who was still watching the soldiers. He saw how engrossed he was with the soldiers combating one another with their swords. Draig went looking for the armorer.

"My good man, would you happen to have a wooden sword that my son could play with?"

"Certainly, sire, wooden swords are one of our most popular toys. What better toy for a child whose father is a soldier?"

"How much are they?" Draig asked.

"They are only a couple of coins. A couple of our soldiers carve them as a hobby when they are not on duty."

Draig handed the armorer the coins and went looking for Drakeson, who was still watching the soldiers practice. Draig walked up behind him and stood there watching. After a few minutes, he tapped Drakeson on the shoulder with the wooden sword.

"Look what I have for you, my son."

Drakeson opened his eyes wide with excitement. The sword was a little large for him as it was really made for a boy of ten or twelve, but that did not slow him down. He took the sword from his father and gripped it in both hands. He then began swinging it wildly, trying to mimic the soldiers. Draig was wondering if getting him a sword was a such good idea after Drakeson nearly hit him four or five times.

Out of a sense of self-preservation, Draig had to explain to his little soldier that one never fights from the seat of a wagon, and so he put the sword under the seat until they got home, explaining that this was where a Roman leaves his sword when on a wagon.

When they pulled up in front of the barn, Drakeson ran for the house to show his mother his new toy. Draig, meanwhile, unloaded the hay and prepared the rest of the kegs of wine for delivery. When he took the supplies into the house, Wilona had a few chosen words for him.

"Why would you give your son such a thing? Do you realize that he has already attempted to kill my left leg, the table, your chair and Lucky twice?"

Draig turned to Drakeson. "When Romans enter the house they leave their sword at the door."

Drakeson went over and set his sword against the wall next to the door and ran off to play in his room. With nothing else to say to Drakeson, Draig looked at Wilona and smiled.

"Problem solved," Draig said. "He just did not know the rules for being a Roman soldier."

Draig left Wilona standing there as he went out to finish his deliveries. Meantime, Drakeson was running around the farm playing Roman soldier.

Early one evening, when Drakeson was eight, Draig saddled Onyxia and brought her out of the barn. He lifted Lucky up into the saddle and then called out to Drakeson:

"Drakeson, come and learn a great lesson."

Drakeson opened the door and ran to his father. Draig helped the young boy into the saddle and climbed on behind him. He called down to Wilona.

"We will not be long, my wife. Only long enough for him to learn about the circle of stones."

"I will have your supper ready when you return." Wilona said.

When they arrived at the circle of stones, Draig took Drakeson down from the saddle and led him into the circle. Drakeson looked up in awe at the massive stones. He put his little hands on the stones and felt their cold, smooth surface.

"Who brought them here, Father?"

"The Great Ones of our ancestors brought them here."

"Why?"

"This is a sacred place to the Great Ones. Come and learn."

They sat down in the center of the stones. Draig looked into his son's eyes and began to tell a story. As Draig told the story,

Drakeson sat wide-eyed and engrossed in the story, hanging on every word and barely blinking.

"In the beginning there was Oneness and all about the Oneness was void. The Oneness was energy encased in firmness. All that was and all that is and all that shall be are part of the one. Deep within the center of the Oneness grew the Spark of Life. And this spark ignited with infinite power sending the Oneness in all directions, ever expanding into the void. And the One became the many. But the many were still in darkness. After a time, one of the many became lonely and thought, 'If I had children to dance about me, I would not be lonely.' So, the one of the many gave birth to children who circled about her like children about their mother. And the one of the many was happy and glowed like a mother among her children, and there was a point of light in the darkness that was the void. The other ones of many saw this and likewise wished to be happy. Soon, the void was filled with the light from the many."

Draig raised his hand to the sky and declared, "Behold the ones of the many."

Looking up at the stars, Drakeson asked, "Is that what the points of light in the sky are, Father?"

"Yes, my son, they are the ones of the many."

"There are so many of them! Do you know all their names?"

"When the sun rises in the morning and warms the earth, she is also one of the many, and we sit on one of her children."

Draig then took Drakeson around the circle of stones and showed him how the celestial events are marked here. He showed him where the summer and winter solstice are marked. He showed him where the spring and fall equinox are marked. He also showed him where the movements of the sun and moon are recorded. He showed him all the events recorded here by the stones.

Once Draig had finished showing Drakeson all the celestial events, he knelt and closely held his son.

"These events are not the only purpose for this site, but it is the purpose that still remains."

They then rode home where Wilona had their dinner waiting for them. Drakeson ran to her in the doorway.

"Did you have a good adventure, my son?" she asked.

"Mother, we saw the circle of stones. They were great and tall they were!"

"Yes, they are! I, too, have stood among the stones."

As Draig came in the door, she said, "Sit down, the both of you. Supper is on the table. Eat before it goes cold."

As they ate their supper Drakeson rambled on about the great adventure. He was so excited he couldn't contain himself. Wilona could only look at Draig and smile. Drakeson talked on and on about the whole trip all through the evening. They had to fight to get him to settle down for the night.

For days that seemed to be without end, Drakeson tried to recite the story of the Oneness. Whenever he got stuck for a word, he would tug at his father's pant leg and repeat the part he remembered.

"And all about the Oneness was void…Oneness was void."

"The Oneness was energy," Draig offered.

"The Oneness was energy encased in firmness," Drakeson continued.

This exchange continued until Drakeson could finally recite the entire tale without any errors. And so it was that Drakeson had learned the lesson of the creation of the universe that his father had learned so many years ago. Other lessons followed. Drakeson listened and learned.

Even at Drakeson's young age, it was still time for Draig to start teaching Drakeson how to hunt. Draig tried to show Drakeson how to shoot his bow, but he was still too small to be able to draw back on the string. This did not mean, however, that he was too young to go hunting, since shooting prey was only a small part of hunting.

Draig taught Drakeson to scan the trees for movement and not just for prey, for there is a more dangerous animal in the forest. That animal is the animal called man. While it is much easier to see large animals moving at a distance, even a small movement of a bush can give a small animal away.

He also taught him how to walk quietly in the forest. Make too much noise and you scare your prey before you can even see them. It also depends on what prey you are hunting, because if you are hunting men, you do not want to give them the advantage of hearing you approach.

As a lesson, Draig stopped and told Drakeson to be very quiet and listen. Soon they heard the loud snap of a twig. They turned to where the sound came from and spied several Roman soldiers walking through the trees. They were terribly clumsy in the forest, as if they were stomping on piles of dried leaves.

Draig also taught him how to read the signs that an animal had passed by. Every animal leaves a different footprint on the ground. You simply had to learn which footprint belonged to which animal. When they returned from hunting, Drakeson had plenty to share with his mother.

One day, Drakeson followed his father into the barn. He finally got curious enough about the kegs that sat in the corner to ask his father about them.

"You put these here, but you never sell them."

"That is because these are not wine. They are a special drink that takes much longer to ferment."

"What is it called?"

"It is called dragon juice."

"Why is it called dragon juice?"

"It is called dragon juice because that is what it has always been called."

"But why?"

"Because that is what the one that taught me how to make it called it."

While it would not have been a satisfactory answer for Wilona, it was a perfectly acceptable answer for Drakeson. Drakeson wandered off to play, and Draig sat down and thought about how long this would be an acceptable explanation.

As Drakeson grew older, he became more involved in the chores about the farm. When Draig would chop firewood, it was Drakeson who would pile the firewood onto the woodpile next to the house. When Draig would bring water from the river to the house, he would carry two large buckets and Drakeson would carry a small pail. Each chore was gauged to Drakeson's ability to perform them.

Drakeson had also reached the age when he was able to help his father carry the offerings brought by the Angeln. Draig would carry one basket while Drakeson would struggle to drag the basket to the house, leaving a long trough on the ground behind him. It would have been easier for Draig to do it himself, but Drakeson enjoyed helping.

As the seasons came and went, Drakeson continued to grow. It would not be long before he would be considered a man in the village Draig came from. Draig would have to find a way to deal with that, but he kept telling himself it would be another day.

Chapter 4

The Secret Revealed

Drakeson had grown into a fine young boy. One day, when he was twelve, Drakeson was playing outside while his father rested in the house. He had the wooden sword that Draig had bought him when he first traveled to Cunetio with him. He was playing one of his favorite games— Romans and Picts. As he battled his imaginary opponents, he slowly made his way into the barn.

Once in the barn, Drakeson hacked down several of his imaginary enemies before he grew wary of the battle. Drakeson saw Onyxia's brush hanging on the post and decided that brushing her might be more fun than playing all alone. He reached for the brush and started grooming Onyxia.

While he brushed Onyxia, he became fixated on the stairs that led to the loft. He had remembered that the loft was forbidden because of the one time in his life that his father yelled at him out of anger. Yet, this did not keep him from wondering what it was up there that he was forbidden to see. This was not the first time that Drakeson had been curious about what was in the loft. It was, however, the first time that he let his curiosity get the better of him.

Drakeson tiptoed to the door and peered out to see if his father had come out of the house. Not seeing him, he assumed he was still resting. Drakeson cautiously began to creep up the stairs, feeling his heart beating fast within his chest and a nervous sweat begin to form on his face. He was scared he would get caught, but he was not going to let his curiosity go unfulfilled.

When he reached the top of the stairs, he stood there and scanned the dimly lit loft. He saw that the loft was empty except for a large chest that rested on the floor next to the wall and three plaques that hung on the wall behind it. As he approached the chest, he saw a series of rings on the floor in front of the right corner of the chest. Upon closer inspection Drakeson realized that they were caused by the bottom of the wine bottle that his father walked up here with each night.

Drakeson stared at the plaques on the wall and read the names that were carved onto each plaque. In a soft voice, he read each name aloud:

"Bellorus."

"Dormanus."

"Melkoran."

He continued to look at the plaques. He had never seen these names before nor had he heard his father mention them. He figured, from the sound of them, that they had to belong to people. He thought they could belong to ancestors, but he had never heard his father speak of them in his lessons. He wondered if they could have been epic warriors, great kings, or perhaps even gods. Since he had no way of learning who they were, he turned his attention to the great chest that sat on the floor before him.

He knelt in front of the chest and put his hands on the large, heavy lid. He began to tremble, not just out of excitement but also out of fear of being caught. Slowly, he lifted the heavy lid and looked inside.

All that he could see was an old blanket that covered the contents. He looked toward the stairs and then looked around the loft as if he expected someone to be standing there behind him. He slowly pulled the blanket away and looked at the contents that the blanket concealed.

As he looked into the chest a golden winged creature stared back at him. The winged creature was not foreign to him. It was the same winged creature as was depicted in the wooden toy he owned. It was the toy that still sat in his room but no longer had been played with for several years.

After closer examination, he saw that it was a most magnificent chest of armor. The armor was silver inlaid with gold, and a winged creature was within a gold emblem emblazoned on the front. The armor was so highly polished that Drakeson could see his reflection as if he was looking into a mirror.

His attention finally turned to an object wrapped in cloth that was wedged between the armor and the front of the chest. He picked up the object and removed the cloth. He held a triangular shield with the same winged creature emblazoned in the center in a circle of gold. In each of the three corners of the shield there were large gemstones that resembled large pearls that glowed.

Drakeson's eyes then fixed on a sheathed sword that lay in the back of the chest. He stood up and lifted the sword from the chest. As Drakeson unsheathed the sword, he opened his eyes wide as they moved from the hilt to the point of the blade. Never in his days had he seen such a marvelously crafted sword. It was definitely better made than any of the Roman swords that he was used to seeing.

Drakeson raised the sword up with both hands. A ray of light from outside struck the blade and lit up the runes that were engraved into the blade, making them glisten in the dimly lit loft. They were like nothing he had ever seen. In his excitement, Drakeson forgot about the rule he had broken and ran for the house, dragging the sword with him.

Draig was sitting in his chair near the fireplace. His eyes were closed, but he was not sleeping. Drakeson burst through the door and ran up to his father. He shook his father's leg and called out as he held up the sword.

"Father, Father, what does it say on this sword?"

Draig opened his eyes and looked at the sword in his son's hands. Filled with anger, he jumped up and grabbed the sword away from Drakeson. Unable to control his anger, Draig yelled at his son.

"I told you to never go into the loft!"

Drakeson cowered and hid his face as he anticipated a well-deserved thrashing, but none came. As he looked up, Draig was standing there with his eyes closed, mumbling to himself.

"Is fabht nadar daonna. Is fabht nadar daonna."

Draig sat down in his chair holding the sword. He held the sword in his hand and ran his fingers across the runes. The look on his face turned from anger into one of sadness. Tears filled his eyes as he sat there silently looking at the sword.

"Father, what does it say on the sword?"

"San ceum mar ri dragon," Draig said.

There was silence as Draig stared at the sword. Drakeson looked to his mother as if to ask her what was wrong. All she could do was shrug her shoulders.

Draig cleared his throat and then explained:

"This sword was a present from a very old friend, and these are words I have not spoken since before you were born."

Drakeson asked, "What do these words mean, Father?"

Trying to fight back tears, Draig's lower lip began to quiver and his hands trembled as he fought back the sadness that had overcome him.

"San ceum mar ri dragon . . . He walks with dragons."

"Dragons are real, Father?" Drakeson asked.

Draig smiled. "They are as real as you and I, my son, and I was honored to walk among them. Alas, they no longer walk among us."

Draig rose from his chair and said, "Come my son, I cannot protect you from my past any longer. I guess it is time for you to learn about who your father once was."

Draig had hoped, all these years, that this day would never come, and yet he knew in the back of his mind that it was as inevitable as the rising of the sun. Until now, Draig was able to hide his past from the world, and now there was little choice but to teach his son of the past that he had lived.

Draig grabbed the bottle of wine from the shelf and began slowly walking toward the barn. Drakeson and Wilona followed close behind. Even Lucky ran after them as if she knew what was going on. Since Draig had never spoken of the days before they met, Wilona was as curious as was their young son.

Draig entered the barn with Wilona and Drakeson a pace behind. Draig stopped halfway up the stairs and turned to his family as Lucky scurried past him.

He took a deep breath and explained to them: "I require a moment of silence when we get to the loft. I have a ritual I must perform to pay respect to some very special friends. As you have waited this long, a few moments should not matter."

Draig then turned and continued to the loft. Wilona and Drakeson stopped at the top of the stairs and watched as Draig stood before the great chest. He set the bottle down on the spot where the series of rings were on the floor. He then laid his sword against the chest.

Draig then brought his palms together and formed a ball of energy between his hands. The ball of energy became a fiery orb. He took the orb into his right hand and held it out in his open palm. Draig let the orb grow bright until the whole loft was bathed in light and then let the orb rise into the air and hover above their heads. Drakeson was amazed by the orb, though Wilona remembered the lesson she had learned many years ago.

Draig took a cup from behind the chest and filled it from the bottle. He then knelt before the chest and raised his cup to the plaques on the wall.

"Bellorus, old friend, I drink to your memory!"

Draig then took a sip from the cup and bowed his head in a moment of silence.

"Dormanus, old friend, I drink to your memory!"

Draig took another sip from the cup and bowed his head in a moment of silence.

"Melkoran, old friend, I drink to your memory!"

Draig took a sip once more from the cup and bowed his head in a final moment of silence. Overcome by sadness, he sat on the chest and cried. He looked at Wilona and Drakeson and motioned for them to approach. As they stood before him, he began:

"I am Draig, son of Anarcher, son of Eafa, son of Eoppa. I was born a son of Man, but I am no longer son of Man. One day, many ages ago, I became Draig the dragonrider."

Drakeson's eyes opened wide. "You are a dragonrider?"

Draig placed his hand on his son's shoulder and smiled.

"My dragon was Draconos. When I was summoned by the Great Ones, he was my teacher first and my friend and companion after."

Wilona and Drakeson both sat down on the floor. They were both wide eyed and excited like little children listening to a fairy tale. The more they became enthralled, the more animated Draig became in the telling.

"In the darkest days of Man's existence, dragons walked among us. Early Man was weak, but dragonkind saw potential in him so they nurtured him that he might survive. They remained in the shadows so that Man would learn to stand on his own and not be relegated to living in the shadow of a master. At times, the Great Ones would choose a son of Man to serve with them. I was one of those sons of Man."

Wilona asked, "You were one of those chosen in those days?"

"Yes, I was one who was chosen in those early days," said Draig.

"And just how long ago were those darkest days of Man?" she queried.

Draig stood there looking past Wilona to the wall behind her. He pondered in his mind what she might say when he answered her question. He was afraid of how she would accept the truth about his past. Yet, he reasoned that there was little else he could do but to answer.

"It was a time before there was a Rome. It was a time before the great pyramids of Egypt. It was a time when what was, what is, and what shall be were one in the same."

Becoming impatient, Wilona asked again, "Just how old are you, my husband?"

Draig cleared his throat and said, "I have lived for a hundred lifetimes, my wife."

Wilona's expressions of excitement gave way to a feeling of dread. She looked down at the floor and then at Draig. Though she was afraid of what he might say next, she finally got up the courage to ask.

"And how many wives have you had in that hundred lifetimes, my husband?"

Draig laughed. "You are my one and only wife. I loved but once before you. Elianna was a girl from my village. We were inseparable until I was called by the mountain. When I returned to our village as the great warrior I had become, but the time for us had passed. She was no longer the little girl I left behind."

Upon hearing that news, Wilona smiled. Despite the fact she was not pleased that Draig was older than she could ever imagine, at least she knew that she shared her husband with only the memory of one young girl. That was much better than to learn that he had loved many women over those years and that she was but one of many.

Drakeson had held his tongue until now, and there were many questions swirling around in his young mind. One question in particular finally surfaced, and so he asked in a very nervous tone:

"Are you an immortal, Father?" Drakeson asked.

Draig said with a smile, "No, my son. There is no such thing as immortality, not even for dragons. This is the last lifetime I shall see."

"You are going to die, Father?"

"Everyone dies, my son. It is merely a matter of when. In my case, I have simply lived many more years and seen more things than most."

"But how could you live that many years?" Drakeson asked.

"We call it *gubrath*, the forever plant. In the begin time it was everywhere. It grew like weeds in a garden. Today, it grows in but one place—the garden of the Great Ones. It is a very special plant, one that has rejuvenating powers. It makes the body forget how old it is. As long as you continue to consume it, it keeps the body from aging."

Wilona asked, "You can no longer consume it?"

"The garden of the Great Ones is no longer on this realm," Draig answered. "I therefore have no choice in the matter."

Content with the knowledge that his father was not going to die in the immediate future, Drakeson's attention turned to the plaques and the names carved upon them.

Pointing to the plaques, Drakeson asked, "Who are those who are named there?"

"Each dragon is born with a dragon stone within his body. The dragon stone is that which holds the dragon's soul to his body. It is also through the power of the dragon stone that a dragon is capable of focusing great magical energies. This is why the dragon stone is the treasure that each dragon guards. When a dragon dies, his stone dies with him, becoming a cold black stone that is similar to a pumice stone. If a dragon makes the decision to relinquish his dragon stone while he still breathes, the dragon dies, but the dragon stone retains all of its power."

Draig opened the chest and pulled out the shield. He touched the stones that were set into the shield and once again he welled up with tears. His lower lip trembled as he looked upon the shield. He then turned to the plaques on the wall.

"Bellorus… Dormanus… Melkoran…they each gave their last breath to place a stone into my shield so that through their sacrifice I might grow more powerful. Through each stone, my magic is amplified tenfold. As long as I remember them, the Great Ones are not truly gone. It is for that reason I come here each night and drink to their memory."

"Are you a magician, father?"

"I am trained in all the schools of dragon magic, the elemental magic of earth, fire, air and water."

Wilona interrupted. "That is why the Angeln believe you are their god?"

"Yes, my wife. When I first encountered the Angeln, it was a party of warriors. At first, I took them by surprise, but they were not surprised long. When they advanced, I loosed a stream of fire over their heads."

"Like you did to me when I pressed you about your past, all those years ago?"

"Yes, my wife . . . just a small example of what dragon magic can do in the right hands."

"And in the wrong hands?" asked Drakeson.

"There is one law I never taught you. The second law says magic must only be used for good. How you use magic determines if you use it for good or cross into darkness and become lost in the shadows. It is a simple choice. You can control magic or you can let magic control you. But if magic controls you, it will pull you into the darkness. The darkness is ruled by jealousy, envy, greed, anger and hatred. And if one gives into those, the spirit is forever lost."

Draig stood up and put his sword and shield back into the chest and covered them with the old blanket. He closed the lid and put his cup back behind the chest. He picked up the bottle and helped Wilona and Drakeson to their feet.

"That is all for now. There is more to my past, but it is getting too late to continue. Let us leave."

The orb faded as they made their way down the stairs. Draig walked to the house in silence while Drakeson and Wilona continued to toss questions at him all the way to the door. Draig said nothing as he went inside and plopped down in his chair.

Before Wilona and Drakeson entered the house, she grabbed him by the arm and whispered:

"Drakeson, talk no more of this today."

"Why, Mother?" Drakeson asked.

"Your father hid his past for a reason. We must trust his judgment. He will tell us when he is ready."

It was eerily quiet the rest of the day. There were lots of stolen glances, but not a word was spoken. Though curiosity was eating Wilona and Drakeson up inside, Wilona knew that to continue prodding Draig for answers would simply make him angry, and making Draig angry was a bad thing.

That night Draig's dreams were filled with memories of his early years. Each dream took place at a different time and represented a different event in his life. His whole life unfolded before him in brief flashes of memories in his dreams. One after another, some were good memories and some were difficult to relive even in a dream.

In the first dream, Draig was but a small boy when he found himself in a dimly lit cavern where shadows abounded. He heard a voice from the darkness:

"The world you have known is no longer. What was and what is is no longer. Your world is now a vastly greater world than you could ever imagine. You will be given knowledge that is far beyond what your forefathers could ever know. You are about to learn a philosophy that has existed since before Man crawled out of the ooze and learned to walk upright. You will be taught the art of warfare on a scale beyond anything Man has yet conceived. You will also learn how the spiritual world is entwined with the physical world. Finally, you will be taught to wield great magic."

Finally, Draig found himself standing on a mountain. He felt the morning chill on his flesh as the sun was slowly rising in the east. As Draig looked around, he saw that he was in the presence of a great multitude of large, ghostly apparitions with human warriors sprinkled among them. They were all talking in whispers. Draig soon became aware that some of the warriors turned into skeletal warriors with swords in their hands. While animated, they appeared disinterested in the events that were beginning to unfold. Suddenly, Draig heard a voice booming from in front of him:

"My children, I have gathered you together here to discuss our future. I have asked that you bring our human brothers because this affects them as well. Man now stands against us, calling for our destruction. We must decide what course we are to take."

Then there was another voice from the multitude: "As I see it, it is not that difficult a decision to make. There are, in fact, only a few options. We can stand and fight, destroying Man in the process. We can run and hide, though there are few places to hide. The other choice would be to do nothing and wait for Man to make the decision for us."

Another voice called out: "When you find a weed in the garden, you cull out that weed. You do not burn the whole garden because of just one weed."

Yet another voice chimed in. "Today it is but one weed in the garden. It does not remain just one weed, however. One weed becomes two. Two weeds become four. Eventually, that one weed becomes the whole garden." And after a pause for effect, he continued. "We can run away and hide, though one day we run out of places to hide. We can stand and fight. And there is no doubt we would win. But one battle becomes two and two becomes four. We would be condemning the whole of Man to destruction one tribe at a time."

The first voice spoke again. "Yes, Samhain, from the time Man first crawled upon this earth we watched him. Even then we found him worthy to take his rightful place among the creatures that walk upon the earth. While hiding in the shadows, we have protected him. We have nurtured him all these many ages. But now Man grows in great numbers and makes war on everything he sees."

Another voice spoke up. "We cannot kill Man, not even just a few weeds, as you say. The Law says we cannot. But we cannot let Man kill us either. What would this world be like without us?"

Again the first voice spoke, "This is but the beginning. As Man continues to grow in great numbers, it is but a matter of time before others turn against us. It is simply the nature of the animal we call Man."

Draig tossed and turned as the dream continued. The longer the dream unfolded the more violent his thrashing became. As he continued to dream, the words continued to flow:

"My children, the choices are not that complicated. We can stand and fight or we can run away. If we do nothing, those same choices remain. We would simply be allowing Man to decide the time and place, but the results are inevitable. There is yet another choice to consider that I hesitate to contemplate. There is a place that we can go that Man can never follow. But there is one factor that cannot be overcome. All must go, or none can go."

Draig suddenly found himself in the mist-filled valley below with a sword in his hand. He wiped blood from his face and stared at the blood that now bathed his hands. He saw a number of warriors lying on the ground at his feet. They were looking up at him and begging for help, and yet he felt totally helpless. As he looked back toward the mountain, he saw a large glowing portal in the sky. The door slowly swung closed.

It was then that Draig's thrashing about caused him to fall out of bed. He lay sprawled out on the floor with sweat dripping from his face and screamed out, "No! Do not go! Do not go!"

The commotion woke Wilona, who sat there trembling in fear as Draig lay on the floor weeping. Between sobs Draig continued to call out in a soft voice:

"Do not go. Please, do not go."

Draig finally calmed down enough to climb back into bed. As he labored to return to sleep, Wilona reached out and held him gently. After a while, Draig's breathing went from heavy and labored to slow and metered. He was soon fast asleep, and he soon began to dream once again.

In the dream he found himself walking through a thick mist. As he emerged from the mist he came face to face with a woman. She was tall and slender, but she had a muscular physique. Her dark black hair was long and straight, reaching down to her waist. She wore a dress made of chainmail that hung down to just above the knee and a red cape that was tapered at the end. A long sword was strapped to her side.

"Draig, son of Anarcher, son of Eafa, son of Eoppa, I am Scathach, teacher of warriors. It is through me that you will learn the art of war. And you will learn."

She took a couple of steps backward, and then commanded, "Come, Draig, attack me!"

Draig lunged at her, and suddenly he found himself lying on the ground looking up at her. Draig got up and lunged at her again. Once again, he found himself lying on the ground looking up at her. After several more attempts, Scathach looked down at him and grinned.

"It is time for the student to become the teacher."

"Pardon me?" Draig said.

"It is time for the student to become the teacher. You must teach your son what I have taught and what you have learned."

"What do you say?" Draig asked.

"You heard me, son of Man," she said, "It is not as if you are dreaming!"

Just then, Draig awoke and quickly sat up. He looked around the darkness of the room, half expecting to see Scathach standing there looking down at him. As he lay back down, he thought about the dream he just had . . . or was it a dream?

The dream seemed so real that it was obviously more than just a dream. Scathach also said it was no dream. He thought that perhaps it was a vision. Surely the vision had to be a message from Scathach, telling him to train his son. That had to be what she meant when she said the student becomes the teacher. He rolled over and went back to sleep.

Draig awoke at the crack of dawn and went out to get his morning chores done. When he finished, he stood between the house and the barn and called out for his son to join him.

"Drakeson, come out here!"

As Drakeson emerged from the house Draig proclaimed, "Drakeson, son of Draig, son of Anarcher, son of Eafa, I am Draig, Dragonrider. I am the teacher of warriors. It is through me that you will learn the art of war. It will take much time to learn, but anything worth learning is worth learning well."

Draig walked into the barn with Drakeson in tow and climbed the stairs into the loft. Draig moved to the far wall. Draig brought his palms together and formed a ball of energy between his hands. The ball of energy became a fiery orb. He took the orb into his right hand and held it out in his open palm, letting the orb grow bright until the whole loft was bathed in light. Then he let the orb rise into the air and hover above their heads. Draig sat down and motioned for Drakeson to draw near.

"It is time to learn the cleansing ritual. It is a ritual to clear the mind and cleanse the spirit. You are to do this each morning when you wake and each evening before you sleep. Sit before me, legs crossed. This is so you are grounded. It is the process of connecting with the earth's energy."

Drakeson stepped within a couple steps of Draig and sat down on the floor. He crossed his legs as he was instructed. He was eager to begin the first of his training, though he did not understand how sitting on the ground was part of warrior training.

"Close your eyes," Draig began. "Place your hands on your knees with palms pointing toward the sky. Take a deep breath and relax. Listen only to the sound of my voice. Nothing exists beyond the sound of my voice. Turn your eyes within, and look deep into yourself. Look deeply until you can see a white light in the center of the darkness. This is the center of your being. Move closer toward the light until you are at the light."

Draig paused for a moment to allow Drakeson time to visualize what he described. Draig then continued:

"Move into the light. As you enter the light, you find yourself on a dirt path in the woods. Look up and see the sunlight breaking through the branches of the trees above. Listen carefully. You can hear a stream flowing past to your left. As you follow the path, you see a tree growing next to the path. Stop at the tree. Reach out and touch the tree. Do not simply touch it. Feel it. Feel the texture of the bark. Know that you cannot only see the tree, but feel it and it is real."

After allowing time for Drakeson to explore the sensation of the tree, Draig continued:

"Continue down the path. As you move further down the path, you hear a waterfall in the distance. As you move further down the path, the sound of the waterfall gets louder and louder. Look to your left and see a waterfall and a clearing beyond. It is not a large waterfall, only slightly taller than you are. Stand in the waterfall and feel the water wash over you. As you look down, you see baskets floating away from you and down the river. These are your troubles and worries. As they slowly float away, you feel calm and rested. Step out of the waterfall and step into the clearing. There is a large boulder in the center of the clearing. Sit on the boulder. Turn your face toward the sun and feel its warmth upon your face. Feel your clothes and see that the sun has dried them. Now, look to the right side of the boulder. You see a large oak chest. Open it and see that it is empty. Look at your body and see great chains wrapped about you. These represent the emotions of Man. One by one, remove them and place them into the chest. While your emotions are in the chest, you will not feel them. They are no longer a part of you. It is now time to return. Leave the clearing and walk the path toward where you came. As you follow the path you see the light once again. Walk into the light. Now, return and open your eyes. You are once again where you began."

Drakeson opened his eyes to find himself sitting on the floor in the loft where he started. He felt fresh and rested. A smile came across his face as he spoke to his father.

"Father, I could actually feel the tree, and when I was in the waterfall I felt the water washing over me. I even felt my wet clothes, heavy and stuck to my body. When I sat on the rock, I could feel the warmth of the sun. How could that be?"

Draig explained: "This place you were at—no one can find except you. It is your secret place. You are alone there and you are safe. It is a place that only exists within your mind, but it is a real place."

Drakeson stood to stretch his legs. He looked at the glowing orb as it continued to hover above his head. Drakeson brought his palms together and mimicked his father's actions, minus the orb. His curiosity begged another question.

"When are you going to teach me to do that?"

"I am not," Draig said. "I was instructed to teach you to be a warrior. I was not told to teach you dragon magic."

"How will I learn it then?"

"You may need to talk to a dragon."

Draig smiled, and then he motioned to Drakeson to sit down in front of him. Draig spoke again.

"Drakeson, I have another lesson for you. Are you prepared?"

"Yes, Father, I am prepared."

"Then place your hands on your knees with palms pointed toward the sky. Close your eyes. Take a deep breath and relax. Listen only to the sound of my voice. Nothing exists beyond the sound of my voice. Focus your mind on the hill fort of Cunetio. Do not simply picture it in your mind, but see it with your eyes and know that you are there."

Drakeson found himself walking in the hill fort. He could see the buildings within the walls. He watched the soldiers going here and there as they went about their duties, wandering in and out of the buildings. He soon realized that the soldiers were ignoring him. He could not understand why they would allow a small boy, even one they knew, to move about unchecked.

Drakeson called out to a passing soldier who walked right past him without saying a word. He was about to take after the soldier to attempt to talk to him again when his father was suddenly standing in front of him.

"They cannot hear you, my son. Nor can they see you. You are only here in spirit form. Your body is still in the loft where you left it. You are like a shadow. You are here, but you are not. This is called astral projection."

Drakeson was beginning to understand what his father meant. As he continued to walk around the hill fort, he saw people going about their business completely oblivious to his presence. If they only knew he was there, Drakeson thought. Suddenly and without warning, Draig struck him and knocked him to the ground. Drakeson lay on the ground looking up at his father and rubbing his shoulder.

"I struck you to teach you a lesson. We are not in the physical world. Nor are we in the spirit world. Rather, we are between the two. We are in the in-between, that space between two realms. The soldiers do not see us because they are in the physical world. But know this: we are not alone. There are things that reside within the in-between that can harm you and even kill you if you are not careful. And if you die here in the in-between, your body also dies. Never forget that."

Helping Drakeson up from the ground, Draig spoke again. "Our visit here is over. It is time to return. You are now returned to your body. Take a deep breath and relax."

Drakeson opened his eyes to find himself returned to the safety of the loft. As he stirred, he became aware of a pain in his shoulder. There was no mark, but he definitely felt sore where his father struck him. He had no idea how there could be pain if they were only there in spirit, but he could not deny there was pain.

After Draig caused the orb to dissipate, he headed down the stairs. Drakeson followed closely behind him. As they left the barn and crossed the yard to the house, Drakeson had more questions.

"Is that all, Father?" Drakeson asked.

"You will go to you room and retrieve your emotions from the chest. This exercise you will repeat every morning and every night for a week."

"But when will you begin to train me as a warrior?" Drakeson pleaded.

"We have begun," Draig answered.

"But we have not done anything yet!" Drakeson exclaimed.

"Have we not, my son?"

"No, Father, we have done no warrior training."

"We have learned the most important lesson of combat," Draig replied.

"What is that?" Drakeson asked.

"Emotions can deceive you and cloud your judgment. Emotions have their place, but they can also make you hesitate, and hesitation can mean death. If you fill yourself with emotions like anger and hate, you can be blinded from reason. Thus emotions can be a bad thing, son of Man. Since Man is an emotional being, you cannot rid yourself of emotions completely, yet this meditation allows one to escape them for short periods of time."

Draig entered the house and sat in his chair to rest. Drakeson climbed the ladder to his room and retrieved his emotions from the chest. He sat there for a spell wondering what this actually had to do with being a warrior. Then again, he knew it was not wise to argue with his father.

After his rest, Draig went out to complete his afternoon chores. Not long after, Drakeson came out to join him. They worked together without saying a word for a short time, but Draig knew his son had questions. He also knew he was not likely to get up the courage to ask.

"I was your age when I was summoned to the mountain." Draig said.

"How long did you train?" Drakeson asked.

"I was no longer a boy when I completed my training."

"Will it take me that long, Father?"

"You will train for the rest of your life, my son. The day you think you have learned everything is the day someone proves that they know something you do not."

"Why did you trade being a warrior for being a winemaker?"

"I am still a dragonrider. The truth is that there is a lot more to being a dragonrider than riding dragons."

Drakeson wandered off while Draig finished his chores alone. Draig knew it would not be easy for his son to learn all that he had to teach, but for Scathach he was willing to try his best. When Draig came in for supper, Wilona had a little smile on her face. Draig knew this meant she had something on her mind. Sometimes it was good and sometimes he lived to regret it.

"What, woman?" Draig said.

"I hear you are going to make a dragonrider out of our son."

"I am starting to teach him to be a dragonrider, but it will not be me who decides if he becomes a dragonrider. I am teaching our son, and he will one day teach his son. And each in their own turn will teach theirs," Draig said.

"Am I going to be a dragonrider, Father?" Drakeson asked.

"Well, for now I train you to be a warrior. It will be decided later if you become a dragonrider."

"How will I know, Father?"

"Trust me, if you become a dragonrider, you will know it."

Drakeson had trouble getting to sleep that night. He could not stop thinking about the prospect of being a dragonrider like his father. Once he finally got to sleep, he dreamed about riding dragons in the sky and swooping down on evildoers and vanquishing them with his mighty sword.

As the next week passed, Drakeson's days began and ended with the meditation. Afterwards he would go out and do his chores and play the rest of the day. The difference now was that he did not play Romans and Picts. Instead, he pretended he was a dragonrider sweeping in to rescue a princess or defeat an evil king. Each night he wondered when his father would continue his lessons.

Drakeson also practiced his astral projections by going to the hill fort at Cunetio and wandering around. He walked in and about the buildings and watched as the soldiers went about their duties. He often wished he could interact with them on some greater level than just watching them.

One morning after practicing his meditation, Drakeson climbed down the ladder from his room. His mother motioned for him to come to the table where a meal was already prepared.

"Your father insisted you eat a meal when you came down."

"Why?" Drakeson asked.

"He did not say and I did not ask. Sit and eat."

Drakeson sat down and quickly ate his meal, being eager to join his father. Just as he finished his meal and rose from the table, he heard his father from outside.

"Drakeson, are you going to spend the entire morning eating?"

Drakeson rushed outside to find his father standing halfway between the house and the barn.

"Yes, Father?"

"Drakeson, son of Draig, son of Anarcher, son of Eafa, attack me!" Draig commanded.

It sounded like a strange request to Drakeson, but he did as he was told and lunged at him. Suddenly, he found himself lying on the ground, looking up at his father. Draig reached down and helped him to his feet.

"Again . . . try again," Draig demanded.

Drakeson lunged at his father again. Once more he found himself lying on the ground looking up at him. Drakeson would not give up. He lunged at his father try after try. Yet, each time he found himself on the ground looking up at his father.

And then Draig asked, "If you are standing at the bottom of a hill and a boulder comes rolling down, what would you do?"

"I suppose that I would step aside?"

"To defend oneself, always remember that you are at the bottom of the hill, and your attacker is the boulder. As he charges you, step aside and allow his own weight to become a tool for you to use. Now it is your turn. Prepare!"

Draig lunged at Drakeson and he tried to step aside, but he was not fast enough, and Draig pushed him down. And there he was, once again, lying on the ground looking up at his father. They repeated this exercise many times, and each time Drakeson was able to perform a little better. After the last attempt, Draig put his hand on Drakeson's shoulder and said,

"Do not worry, my son, I was no better than you on my first day of training."

"How long will it take for me to train, Father?" Drakeson asked.

"As long as it takes you to learn," Draig said, giving his son a grin. "Each learns at their own pace. I can promise that it will be a very long time, son of Man."

Draig chuckled as he walked off to the barn. He remembered how someone spoke those exact words a very long time ago. Indeed, the student had become the teacher.

Drakeson called after his father. "Father, why do you call me 'son of Man'?"

Draig turned to him and said, "I did not notice. I guess it is because that is what my teacher called me when I was learning. It was meant as a term of endearment."

Drakeson ran off to play before his afternoon chores. He also thought about what his father had said. He then repeated it out loud over and over.

"son of Man…son of Man…son of Man."

At first, he thought it sounded more like an insult than a term of endearment, but then after he said it a few more times, he decided that it was not so bad to be called son of Man.

Each morning Drakeson woke up and ate a hearty meal, and each morning he would step outside to find his father waiting for him. Draig continued to charge him and knock him to the ground. Finally, to Drakeson's surprise, his father was lying on the ground looking up at him.

"Is it not better to be the one looking down for a change?"

"Yes, Father, it is much better!"

They both laughed as Draig got up from the ground. He brushed himself off and started walking toward the barn. Drakeson ran after him.

"Where are you going?"

"Where are we going, you mean. It is one thing for Romans to see us wrestling. It is another thing to see us actually training."

They climbed into the loft. Draig brought his palms together and formed a ball of energy between his hands. The ball of energy became a fiery orb that he took into his right hand and held out in his open palm. Draig let the orb grow bright until the whole loft was bathed in light, and then he let the orb rise into the air and hover above their heads.

Draig began with hand to hand combat, teaching Drakeson all about defensive techniques. He taught him all about blocking and parrying blows. They repeated the exercises until Drakeson had fully grasped every nuance of defending himself. The training eventually included disarming attackers armed with an array of weapons. With each day Drakeson felt more comfortable with his skills.

Not until Drakeson had learned all there was to learn about defensive techniques did Draig begin to teach him offensive skills. They started with jabs and right crosses and progressed to hooks and uppercuts. Draig also taught him several techniques using his feet and legs. They practiced these techniques until Drakeson mastered them all.

One morning, Drakeson rose and went out to the barn to find that Draig had harnessed Onyxia to the wagon and left. He was curious why he would leave without waiting for him. He ran into the house.

"Where did Father go?" he asked his mother.

"He left early this morning for the hill fort of Cunetio. He went to get a load of hay for Onyxia as well as to purchase foodstuffs to supplement the garden."

"Why did he not wake me to go with him?"

"He did not say and I did not ask," Wilona said.

Drakeson went outside to do some light chores about the farm. He was rather upset that his father would leave without asking him to go along, but he did wake up a bit late. He could only assume his father did not want to disturb his sleep.

Hay and foodstuffs were not the only reason Draig went to Cunetio. While there, Draig went to find the praefectus fabrum to purchase two wooden practice swords and shields. It seemed a strange request, so the praefectus questioned Draig.

"Why would a farmer require practice swords?"

"My son has outgrown his old toys, and I wished to purchase new ones for him."

"But why does he require two swords and shields?"

"On our trips to Serum, I sometimes take my son. Once, we encountered a traveler who talked about warriors in a distant land and who had fought with two swords, one in each hand."

This explanation was acceptable to the praefectus, and so he allowed Draig to purchase the swords and shields. Draig slipped them under the seat and rode home. When Draig arrived at the farm, he snuck the swords and shields into the loft and unloaded the wagon.

The next day, when Drakeson came out to practice, Draig led him into the loft in the barn. The moment they reached the loft, Drakeson was surprised when he noticed the wooden practice swords leaning against the chest. Draig picked them up and handed one to Drakeson.

"Why are we playing with toys, Father?"

"These are not toys. Do you not remember seeing Roman soldiers at Cunetio using them to practice?"

"Yes, Father, but why do we not use real swords?"

"If I were to cut off your ear while practicing, you might understand why we use these instead. What's more, if you are not paying attention, these wooden swords will cause pain."

Draig spent hours teaching Drakeson to parry and dodge. He also taught him to block blows. At first, the blows Draig delivered were soft and easy to defend, but as time passed the blows came harder and faster. After hours of practicing defense, Drakeson became impatient.

"When am I going to start learning to attack?"

"Patience, my son. You do not last long on a battlefield if you cannot keep those who oppose you from striking you down."

"Yes, Father, as you command."

Once Drakeson became proficient in defending himself against attacks with a sword, they progressed to sword and shield strategy. The more they practiced the better Drakeson was able to fend off Draig's blows.

Unfortunately, Drakeson was getting a little too cocky for his own good. Draig saw this and quickly delivered two quick blows to fade Drakeson out of position. He then spun around and hacked at the back of Drakeson's legs and knocked him to the floor.

"Keep your head on what you are doing or you will lose your head."

Draig took the swords and laid them up against the wall where he originally got them.

"That is enough for the day," he said.

When they came down the stairs, Draig picked up Onyxia's brush and began brushing her coat. Drakeson stopped and watched for a few minutes. He finally turned to leave the barn.

"Why do we use sticks in the loft instead of taking advantage of the open grounds outside?" Drakeson asked.

"Because Romans become a bit nervous when they see farmers using swords, and you've seen enough Romans to know they pass our farm on a regular basis."

"Yes, Father."

As he stepped out of the barn door, Draig called after him. "The Romans must not know that I am trained in combat. If they were to know I was so trained, they would wonder who trained me. They cannot know what I am. They must not know what you are becoming. You must trust that I know what is best for us all."

Drakeson went into the house as Draig continued to brush Onyxia. Though he knew that Drakeson was impatient, he also knew that an impatient warrior often becomes a dead warrior.

Time passed and Drakeson became more proficient in the use of swords. While he still required practice, he had learned all the techniques that Draig had available to him.

One morning as Drakeson joined his father in the loft, he noticed that there were too large tree branches lying against the chest. They were stripped and roughly five feet long. Draig handed his son one of the makeshift staves.

"It is time to learn the use of the staff," Draig said.

"These are not staves; they are large sticks!" Drakeson demanded.

"Were not the wooden practice swords just toys? And you still learned to use them just the same."

"Yes, Father. I apologize for speaking out." Drakeson said.

"No need to apologize. Even a dragonrider has an opinion. One is merely required to know when to voice that opinion. Now come and learn the noble art of the staff."

Draig stepped back to give him room, and then he began to rotate the staff in a circular motion. At first, he rotated the staff very slowly so that Drakeson could see exactly how he was rotating it, but he gradually increased the speed until the staff was but a blur.

"It is said that a spinning staff can stop an arrow from the most proficient bowman. I have not yet tested that claim. Perhaps there are those who are braver than I who will one day find out."

Drakeson tried his hand at spinning his makeshift staff. He was good at spinning it slowly, but as he tried to spin it faster, he lost control and sent the staff flying. Each time he dropped the staff he simply reached down and picked it up to try again.

Draig then began to spin the staff in a figure eight pattern from his left side to his right side. Again, he began very slowly so that Drakeson could see the mechanics of the action. He then sped up the rotations so that it again became a blur. Suddenly, Draig stretched his arm, and the one end of the staff stretched out from his hand as the other end ran tightly along his arm.

"With this technique I have two options. I can either reach out like this and strike at an opponent's head, or reach out low and strike his legs in an attempt to knock him off his feet."

As Drakeson attempted this new technique, Draig tried to find a safe corner in which to hide in. In his first attempt, Drakeson rotated the staff too far and struck himself in the back of the head. The amusement of this was not lost on Draig, who laughed out loud. As Drakeson continued to try, he became better with each attempt.

Drakeson asked, "Why would one use a staff instead of a sword?"

"The staff is known as the poor man's weapon," Draig explained, "because even the poorest man can afford a stick. It is also the weapon least likely to cause alarm if one is seen walking with it as it is common among monks and commoners for use as a walking stick."

Drakeson thought a moment. "So, the staff is a weapon that is hidden in plain sight?"

"A rock is only a rock until you pick it up and throw it at someone," Draig explained.

Over the following days, Draig taught Drakeson the techniques of combat with the staff. They practiced staff against staff and sword against staff. As Drakeson became more proficient in using the staff, Draig showed him the subtle differences between the staff, the pike, and the spear. The main difference between the staff and the other weapons were their length and the added weight at one end.

It was now time to teach Drakeson to use a bow. This would be easier since Drakeson had already gone hunting with his father. There was little difference in shooting at a stag to provide meat for the table and shooting at a man.

Draig made a trip to Serum and purchased a bow for Drakeson. Since this was a weapon with which Drakeson would have to practice outside, he then made him targets that resembled animals. He made a squirrel, a rabbit, and a red deer. They were all life-size. He reasoned correctly that passing soldiers would simply consider that Drakeson was learning to hunt.

When Draig made a target that resembled a bear, he made the bear stand on his hind legs so that the target's shape most resembled a man with his hands held up above his head. Draig knew that passing soldiers would simply see the target as a bear and not make the leap to recognize that it resembled a man.

Soon Drakeson had learned the techniques of each of the weapons, and now he needed to practice what he had learned. From that point forward they would do their morning chores and then spend two hours practicing combat in the loft.

Draig knew that it would take Drakeson years to master the skills of a dragonrider, but at least now he had the knowledge. It was now simply a matter of practicing what he learned.

Chapter 5

No Such Thing as Immortality

As Draig sat in his chair one night, he thought back to when he was in his village so many years ago. He had seen the leaves on the trees turn brown twelve times. He remembered how he was looking forward to the first time he would go hunting with the men, for this was the tradition. This was the first major milestone in a young boy's life as it was the first symbol that he was becoming a man.

He realized that Drakeson had also seen the leaves turn brown twelve times. If Draig had remained in his village and never left to become a dragonrider, Drakeson would now be becoming a man in the tradition of his ancestors in the village. Draig could not let this tradition die. He owed it to his son to preserve their heritage, the old as well as the new.

He had to mark this time in some special way. Drakeson had been going hunting with him since he was very young, so simply taking him hunting would not be sufficient. He would have to get him a present that both represented this time in his life and be something useful as well.

Draig thought about this present for several days without coming up with a satisfactory gift. One day, while thinking about Drakeson's present, he finally came up an idea. It was not simply an idea, it was an excellent idea. It was both traditional and useful. It was the perfect gift.

Draig went out and found himself a grove of yew trees. He searched for hours, looking for the perfect sample of yew wood to suit his purpose. He finally came upon an ancient yew tree that called to him. It was not as old as Draig was, but it had seen a good deal of his lifetime. He cut the piece of wood out of the living yew tree and carried it home. When he arrived back at the farm, he hid the wood in the loft.

Each day, he spent time slowly carving the piece of wood. It was not long before he had finished carving the most marvelous gift. There was but one problem that remained: the wood was still wet and it would take considerable time to dry thoroughly. For anyone else this might have appeared to be a large problem, but Draig was not just anyone.

Draig brought his palms together and drew in the treoir. He formed a ball of energy between his palms and let the ball of energy become a fiery orb. He blew gently on the orb, and a ball of hot air formed and enveloped the wood. Wisps of steam rose as the wood dried from the inside out as it also dried outside in. Soon the wood was thoroughly dry, and Draig allowed the orb to dissipate.

Draig placed Drakeson's present on the chest and made his way down to the house. It was supper time, so the present had to wait a little while. Draig was excited, but he had to hide his excitement until the meal was finished.

"My son is becoming a man. It is right that we honor this time in your life as would our ancestors. The problem is that if I had not become a dragonrider, we would still be in the village and we would have marked that day by you going on your first hunting trip."

"But I have already been hunting. We have gone hunting many times since I was but a small boy," Drakeson said.

"Yes, my son, it is much too late for that experience to mark this time in your life, but I have thought of another way. Come, follow me to the loft."

Draig rose and walked toward the barn with Drakeson and Wilona following close behind. As they reached the barn and began to climb the stairs to the loft, Draig stopped.

"Close your eyes that you shall not see what I have prepared."

Drakeson closed his eyes, and his mother aided him in climbing the remaining steps into the loft. Draig stood him in the middle of the loft and faced him toward the chest.

"Kneel and prepare, my son." As Drakeson knelt, Draig brought his palms together and formed a ball of energy between his hands. The ball of energy became a fiery orb. He took the orb into his right hand and held it out in his open palm. Draig let the orb grow bright until the whole loft was bathed in light and then let the orb rise into the air and hover above their heads.

Draig then placed the gift in his son's hands. As Drakeson opened his eyes, he saw that he was holding a longbow. But it was not just a longbow; it was a work of art. The bow was slightly smaller than a normal longbow because of Drakeson's size, but the quality of the bow was no less superior.

"Drakeson, son of Draig, son of Anarcher, son of Eafa, by the traditions of our ancestors you are now a man. This bow is a sign of your manhood."

They then left the loft and went into the house. Drakeson slept with the bow at his side that night. He was so thrilled to be honored with such a marvelous weapon.

Drakeson spent days practicing with his new longbow. It was hard to draw back, but that did not stop him from becoming accurate with it. As Draig watched his son practice, he noticed that Drakeson treated the longbow as an ordinary bow and he had to do something about it.

Standing next to Drakeson, Draig asked, "Are your eyes bothering you, my son?"

"No, Father, why do you ask?"

"You are standing so close to the targets. I thought you were having trouble seeing."

"But I set my targets at a full seventy-five paces, Father."

It is true that seventy-five paces was a great distance, but this was only half the distance that a longbow could reach. Draig backed his son up another seventy-five paces. Standing a full two hundred yards from the targets, Drakeson did not know if he could hit the targets so very far away.

Drakeson pulled back and took careful aim. He let an arrow fly, half expecting the arrow to drop short of the target. He did miss the target, but the arrow struck the tree behind it. Drakeson began practicing from this new distance and found his accuracy improved rapidly.

One morning, Draig picked up his bow and stepped outside. As he looked around, it was no surprise to him that Onyxia was already prancing around the farm with Lucky on her back. Draig whistled loudly and then called out:

"Who wants to go hunting?"

"I do, Father!" Drakeson said as he emerged from the house.

Drakeson ran to get his bow as Onyxia walked over to where Draig was standing with Lucky still on her back. The party was assembled and began to head south. After only a few paces, Draig looked back to see that Onyxia and Lucky had stopped at the edge of the farm.

Draig called back to them, "You are not coming?"

Onyxia turned her head to look at Lucky and then looked back at Draig. She then turned around and went back to wandering around the farm with Lucky still on her back. It was obvious that they were not interested in hunting.

"Come, Drakeson, I guess it is just you and I today."

They continued to head south until the farm disappeared into the distance. Draig was less talkative than usual; he was still preoccupied thinking about Onyxia and Lucky not wanting to come along. While it was not unusual for Onyxia to stay at the farm, it was highly unusual for Lucky to skip a hunting trip.

"What are we hunting for today?" Drakeson asked.

"Well, the other day your mother mentioned that she was craving a nice rabbit stew, so I guess we should get her a couple plump rabbits."

"What if we run across a nice red deer?"

"We will just have to remember where he was for the next time we go hunting."

Just then, Draig caught sight of a rabbit about two hundred yards away. He put his hand on Drakeson's shoulder and pointed in the direction of the rabbit.

"There, do you see it?"

Drakeson stopped and scanned the ground ahead until he saw the rabbit. It was just sitting there nibbling on a plant, oblivious to the world around it. Drakeson cocked an arrow and took aim. He let the arrow fly and the rabbit rolled over and over when the arrow struck.

"Good shot, young dragonrider!" Draig shouted.

Drakeson ran and picked up the rabbit and tied it to a length of twine and slung it over his shoulder. They continued their search for a second rabbit. As they continued walking, Drakeson thought about Onyxia and Lucky.

"You seem bothered that Onyxia and Lucky did not want to come with us," Drakeson said.

"We used to spend so much time together, but these past few years we have spent much less time. These last few weeks they seem to be even more distant," Draig said.

"Why do you think that is, Father?"

"I do not know, my son."

"Do you think it is my fault?" Drakeson sheepishly asked.

"Why would you say such a thing?" Draig asked.

"There was not a problem between you and them until I came along." Drakeson said.

"Never think that your birth was anything but a joyous event for all of us. They paced all night with me the night before you were born. They were present at the circle of stones when I named you. Has not Lucky been in the loft most every step of your training?"

"Are you sure, Father?" Drakeson asked.

Draig did not answer. Drakeson knew this meant his father had spoken his final word on the matter. This meant it was best to not press him any further. As they continued to head south, Drakeson limited the conversation to small talk, and Draig was more than willing to comply.

They continued to hunt, making a large circle and heading back toward the north. It had taken them most of the morning already, and they still had but one rabbit to show for their efforts. This also gave Draig more time to think about Onyxia and Lucky, and it was not long before he thought out loud.

"I know where there are some crabapples," Draig said. "I think I'll collect some up for Onyxia. Maybe she just needs a good treat to make her feel better."

Draig altered their path through the woods to take them to the crabapple trees from which he had so often foraged. As they approached the area of the crabapple trees, Drakeson spotted a second rabbit running across their path. Drakeson quickly drew back on his bow and let fly an arrow, striking down the rabbit in mid-stride.

Drakeson tied the second rabbit to the first one and slung them over his shoulder. They then continued on to the crabapple trees.

Draig pulled a small bag that he had stored in his shirt and stuffed a dozen juicy crabapples into the bag, which he swung back and forth as they walked home.

When they got back to the farm, Drakeson took the rabbits to his mother in the house while Draig went to the barn with the crabapples. Draig pulled one of the crabapples from the bag and held it out in his open hand.

"Onyxia, look what I have for you."

Onyxia turned and sniffed at the air. She slowly walked over to Draig and took the crabapple from his hand. He stroked her neck as she chewed her special treat.

"I thought you deserved a nice treat," he said.

When she finished that one, Draig pulled out another from the bag and held it out to her. She took this one from his hand as quickly as she had taken the first one.

When she finished the second crabapple, Draig pulled a third from his sack. Onyxia looked at it, took a good sniff at it and then turned and walked away. Draig was totally stunned.

"You are stopping at just two? I thought you had a whole extra stomach just for crabapples?"

Draig dumped the remaining crabapples into a tub and placed it near the door. As he walked out the door, he turned back to Onyxia and called out to her.

"They are there when you want them."

Draig went into the house and left Onyxia to her crabapples. It seemed odd to him that she did not eat them all at once. A dozen crabapples is usually just a small snack to her. He could only assume she had grazed too much while they were out hunting and was feeling full.

The next day, Draig came out to the barn to begin his chores. He looked into the tub to find that all the crabapples were still there. Draig thought this was odd, so he walked to the door and looked about the farm. There they were—Onyxia walking around the farm with Lucky on her back. Everything as it should be, he told himself, and off he went to do his chores.

For the next couple of days, Draig came out to the barn and looked in the tub to find the crabapples were still uneaten. He had also noticed that Lucky had not been coming in at night. Instead, she was sleeping in the barn, a place where she had never slept since the house was built.

Draig thought that perhaps Onyxia was ill, but he noted that Onyxia and Lucky still rode around the farm together each day. He finally told himself that everything was fine. Draig decided that Onyxia was simply saving the crabapples for another day or that she was watching her weight.

Draig woke early one morning and walked outside to begin his chores. As he looked around, he realized something was not quite right, but he could not put his finger on what it was. It finally dawned on him that Onyxia was not prancing around the farm and Lucky was not outside either.

Draig thought this was odd, since they were both usually out and about at first light. He suddenly got a lump in his throat and had a terrible premonition that something was terribly wrong. Draig bolted for the barn and threw open the door.

As he looked into the barn, he saw Onyxia lying motionless on the ground. As he slowly moved closer, his eyes focused on a small lump near Onyxia's neck. It was Lucky, and she was in her favorite place, at the front of where the saddle would have been. They had obviously passed away during the night.

"Draig yelled, "No! It is not fair!"

Draig dropped to his knees and wept for his friends who had passed. After a moment he felt a hand on his shoulder and heard a familiar voice from the past.

"Whoever said that life was supposed to be fair?"

Draig looked up to see a man in a long flowing beard and hair that had long turned gray. He also carried a staff with a polished quartz crystal imbedded at the crown. He wore a dark blue robe fastened at the waist with a gold braided rope whose ends reached to his knees.

"I saw this ripple in the pool that is your life, and I came because you are in need."

"Why, Myrddin?" Draig asked softly.

"Have you forgotten so soon, my friend?" Myrddin said. "There is no such thing as immortality…"

"Not even for dragons," Draig interrupted.

"They were not just animals," Myrddin said. "They were your friends. You meant more to them than you can imagine."

"But I did not even get to say good-bye to them," Draig said.

"They knew their time was drawing near. They chose this way."

"But why did they not tell me?" Draig asked.

"They did not want you to have to stand by and watch them slowly fade away and die. They chose this as the easier way . . . for them and for you."

It was then that Drakeson and Wilona came out of the house, having heard the commotion. As they neared the barn they could see the tears running down Draig's face. They knew something had to be horribly wrong to make Draig cry. Draig put out his hands to stop them.

"Do not come closer," Draig said.

"What is wrong, my husband?"

"Onyxia and Lucky are no longer among us. They passed away while we slept."

Both Wilona and Drakeson started crying. "Are you all right, my husband?" Wilona asked through her tears.

"No, but there is little anyone can do about it."

"This is not an easy thing for you, Draig. Do you want me to take care of them for you?" Myrddin asked.

"No," Draig said, "They were my friends, my family. I owe it to their memory to deal with it myself."

"Where do you want to put them?" asked Myrddin.

Draig pointed toward the oak tree, "They would like to lie beneath the oak tree. They would have shade in the summer and protection from the rain in the winter. They would be happy there."

Myrddin turned to Drakeson. "Get your father a shovel from the barn. We can at least do that for him."

Draig and Myrddin went over to the old oak tree while Drakeson went after a shovel. When Drakeson returned with the shovel, Draig began digging the holes. Myrddin sat down on the bench nearby and watched his friend with his labor of honor. Drakeson knelt and watched his father. For the next few hours there was not a single word spoken. Drakeson noted to himself just how deafening the silence was. This was not like his father at all.

Tears streamed down Draig's face as he dug the two holes for his two friends. It took several hours for him to dig the holes alone, but he wanted to do it himself. It was a matter of honor and respect for his friends. He would have it no other way. When he finished digging the graves, he climbed out of the hole and slumped down on the bench totally exhausted. Myrddin placed a hand on his shoulder to comfort him.

"Rest, my friend . . . this next part is for us to do," Myrddin said as he turned to Drakeson. "Come, bring out the hand cart I saw in the barn and follow me."

Drakeson ran into the barn and pulled the small hand cart and joined Myrddin at the edge of the farm. The pair traveled to an area where there was a large supply of sandstone. Drakeson did not know why they were doing it, but he knew that Myrddin had a reason for it.

Myrddin brought his palms together and drew into his palms the energy known as the treoir. He let the treoir form a ball of energy, and the ball of energy became an earthen orb. Myrddin then released the earthen orb into the sandstone and caused great pieces to break off. They began loading the pieces into the cart.

"You are a dragonrider too!" Drakeson said.

"I was…once upon a very long time ago."

"What happened? Why are you not a dragonrider now?"

"My dragon Atur died. In my heart I could not bring myself to replace him."

"What is all this rock for, Myrddin?"

"You will see soon enough."

Once the hand cart was full, they labored to return to the farm with their cargo. When they arrived at the oak tree, Myrddin and Drakeson emptied the contents of the cart onto the ground. Myrddin then laid some of the sandstone into the bottom of each grave.

"What is that for, Myrddin?" asked Drakeson.

"You will see soon enough."

Myrddin turned to Draig, "We are ready, my friend."

Draig nodded and then rose and walked to the barn. After a moment, he came out carrying Lucky's motionless body in his arms. He gently laid her into the grave that was dug for her. All three of them went in to fetch Onyxia's body. They pulled her onto the hand cart, so as to pull her to the oak tree. Together, they slid her into her open grave and moved the cart away. Myrddin and Draig covered their bodies with the rest of the sandstone.

"Why are we doing this?" asked Drakeson.

Myrddin smiled. "Watch, young one, and be amazed."

Myrddin brought his palms together and drew in the treoir. He let the treoir form a ball of energy, and the ball of energy became an orb of fire. He then held the fiery orb in his right hand and let it grow bright. He slowly released the fire into Onyxia's grave.

Slowly, the sandstone changed from sandstone into quartzite, a clear type of quartz. When Myrddin finally ceased, it was as if Onyxia was encased in a giant clear crystal. He then repeated the process on Lucky. Both animals were encased in tombs that would be forever protected from the elements.

Myrddin and Drakeson went to the river to gather two large stones and brought them to the farm as Draig covered the tombs with dirt. When the pair returned from the river, they laid the stones on the ground.

Myrddin once again brought his palms together and drew into his palms the energy known as the treoir. He let the treoir form a ball of energy, and the ball of energy became an orb of fire. Myrddin took the orb of fire in his right hand and released small balls of fire which cut into the stones that he had brought from the river. Slowly, these stones became carved headstones, one stone for Onyxia and one for Lucky.

Myrddin and Drakeson set the stones in place as Draig stood before the graves of his friends. It brought back memories of when they dug the graves for their fallen comrades not so many years ago.

"The last time we dug graves it changed the whole world. This time we dug graves and it only changed my life. I cannot tell you which one hurts the most.

With Onyxia and Lucky laid to rest, Myrddin sat down on the bench and spoke to Draig:

"Draig, sit and listen to what I have seen with my mind. Know they felt no pain when they passed. Also know that they were not alone when their time came."

"He came for them?" Draig asked.

"Yes, Draig, he was here with them in their final moments. He had to be here to collect their spirits and take them back with him. Their spirits are with Draco, now and forever."

"It is a warm feeling to know they are not alone." Draig said.

"Draco watches over their spirits as he watched over them in life. Draig, take my hand and close your eyes. See what I see and know it is real."

Draig took Myrddin's hand and closed his eyes. He looked into the darkness within his mind. Slowly, the darkness gave way to the light, and he could see Onyxia prancing in a field. As he looked closer, he saw Lucky riding on her back as she so often did in life. A single tear rolled down his face.

Draig opened his eyes. "Thank you, Myrddin, old friend. It takes a great weight off my heart to see that they are happy."

Myrddin rose. "It is time for me to leave. Remember that whenever you have need of me, I will know, and I will come to you just as I have done today."

Myrddin walked to the edge of the farm and stopped. He looked back at Draig sitting on the bench. He wished he could have remained longer, but he had other pressing matters to which he must attend. He disappeared into the distance.

Draig was comforted that he had such a friend as Myrddin in such a time of need. It made the whole experience that much easier to deal with. Draig sat on the bench near his friends until late that night. He then rose and walked into the house.

The next day, while Draig was still feeling very depressed about the loss of his friends, he forced himself to go out to the barn to begin his chores. Standing at the doorway, he looked down at the tub that was still filled with the crabapples he had collected days before. He sat down and picked up one of the crabapples.

"What I do now I do for you, Onyxia," he whispered.

He then began to eat the crabapple. As he finished eating the crabapple, he collected the seeds and placed them in the pile. He then picked up the next crabapple and began to eat it as well. Tears once again filled his eyes as he continued eating the crabapples, one after another.

Once he finished the crabapples, he collected up all the seeds and went out to plant them beside the barn. In Draig's mind, this was so that if the spirit of Onyxia happened to come by the farm, she would find herself a treat.

A few more days passed, and on the night of the full moon Draig was slowly returning to his chores, though he was still depressed about the loss of his friends. Drakeson had noticed that Draig did not go out for the Angeln offering. It was as if he did not even realize it was the full moon.

Drakeson decided to go out to collect the two baskets of offerings. Because he still wasn't old enough to carry both baskets, he dragged the baskets by their handles all the way from the edge of the clearing and into the house.

Once inside, Drakeson started digging through the baskets to see what the Angeln had given as their offering for the month. In the first basket he found a variety of wild fruits and vegetables. As he dug through the second basket he found something he had not expected.

"Father," Drakeson said, "I do not understand."

"What is it that you do not understand?" Draig asked.

Drakeson reached into the basket and pulled out two wildcat kittens. He held them out, one in each hand, and asked:

"What are these for?"

Draig reached out and took the two kittens from his son and placed them in his lap. He looked them over to see that they were young and healthy.

"Can we keep them, Father?"

"Obviously the Angeln noticed that their god was sad at the loss of his pets and decided to attempt to replace one of them as best they could."

The kittens brought back memories of when Lucky was but a kitten. Once again, tears welled up in his eyes. While the kittens could never replace Lucky, it was still a kind gesture that could not be ignored. Draig quickly realized that one was male and one was female.

Holding up the male, he said, "This feisty little fellow shall be Tyron. He was a great dragonrider who sacrificed himself to protect others."

Holding up the female he said, "This sweet thing shall be Elianna, the girl I knew from my childhood."

Draig smiled for a moment and then placed the two kittens on the floor. Draig then rose up and walked into his room and went to sleep while Wilona went looking for something for the kittens to eat.

"Is Father not happy to receive the kittens?" Drakeson asked.

"You know he likes the kittens," Wilona said, "because he named them, but they also make him sad because they bring back memories of Lucky. Memories can sometimes be painful."

Over the next few days it was becoming obvious that these kittens were not going to be a replacement for Lucky. But Draig could see that they were bonding with Drakeson, and so Draig was actually pleased, as this meant he did not have to be torn between the new kittens and his loyalty to Lucky.

One day a Roman patrol passed the farm. A mounted captain led a dozen men on foot. They also had with them a wagon of supplies, along with a horse tied to the back of the wagon. They stopped and looked for the wildcat that rides the horse, but they were not there. Seeing Draig working in the field, the captain became curious, and so he rode down to the farm while the rest of the patrol remained at a distance.

"Excuse me sir, some of my men are new to our post. They have heard the other soldiers talk of the wildcat that rides a horse. They were hoping to see for themselves. May I ask where they are?"

Tears welled up in Draig's eyes as he pointed toward the oak tree and the graves that lay beneath it. The Roman captain got down off his horse and walked over to the tree and knelt before the graves. After a moment he returned to Draig.

"I have often passed your farm, and each time I would stop and watch them wandering about. It always made me smile. I am sorry for your loss."

"Thank you, captain, you words touch my heart."

The captain mounted and rode back to the patrol. He sat quietly in the saddle as he looked back toward the farm. One of the new soldiers finally spoke up.

"Captain, where is the wildcat that rides the horse?"

"They died a few days ago. I am afraid you will not be seeing them. I am sorry."

The captain sat there looking at the horse that was tied to the back of the wagon. He then looked at Draig working in the field. As the others watched, he untied the horse and quickly rode back to where Draig was standing.

"Sir, one of our officers returned to Rome, and there was no room for his horse. He reluctantly left it with us, but we have little use for a horse without his rider. I would like to give you this horse to replace the one you lost. I am sure the officer would approve of the gesture."

"Thank you, Captain, I appreciate your kindness," Draig said as he took the rope from the captain.

The captain said with a smile, "How would you bring your fine wine to our fort if you do not have a horse to pull your wagon?"

Draig watched as the captain rejoin his troops and away they moved and disappeared. He looked around to see Drakeson standing nearby watching.

Holding out the rope, he called to Drakeson: "Make yourself useful and take the horse to the barn."

Taking the rope from his father, Drakeson asked, "What are you going to name him?"

"He is just a horse. He does not need a name."

Drakeson turned toward the barn and rolled his eyes once he was a few paces away, but only because his father could not see him do it. He wondered why his father was willing to name the wildcat kittens and not the horse. After all, one animal is the same as another in that respect.

That evening, Draig climbed into the loft in the barn to toast to his friends. As he finished his toasts, the loft began to grow brighter, and he heard that same familiar voice he has heard so many times before.

"Why did you not name the horse?"

"What was that?" Draig asked.

"I asked why you did not name the horse."

"He is only a horse," Draig answered.

"The Angeln did not give you the kittens to replace Lucky, nor did the Romans give you the horse to replace Onyxia. By naming them, you do not dishonor the memories of those who have passed. But what about the honor of those who remain?"

"You are right, spirit of Draco. I will honor the new horse by giving him a name. He is a horse and he is brown, so I will call him Echann."

"Now, for my reason for coming, do you know what day approaches?"

"Well, yes, of course," Draig answered. "It is the first day of the new year. It is the Day of the Dead, that one day when the portal opens between this world and the Otherworld so that those who have died during this year may pass to the Otherworld."

"You should take Drakeson to Annwn and teach him about this day and the role we once played in it."

"But how will we get there, spirit of Draco? It is not as if we can fly there."

"You shall make your way to the coast and wait for one of the 'Bag on Noz,' the ghostly ferries. Trust that the ferryman will allow you passage."

"As always, my friend, I will do as you ask."

As Draig bowed his head, the room grew dimmer, and the spirit of Draco vanished as quickly as it had appeared. Draig picked up his wine bottle and made his way to the house.

"Drakeson, come to me and learn."

"Yes, Father?" Drakeson said as he came up and sat on the floor in front of Draig.

"It will soon be the Day of the Dead. It is that day when the spirits of those who have passed during the year make their way to the Otherworld. We have been summoned to stand guard at the portal to the Otherworld on the Isle of Annwn."

"We are going to the Isle of the Dead? How will we get there, Father?" "We will use a Bag on Noz, a ghost ferry. The spirit of Draco told me the ferryman will permit us passage."

"What will we see there, Father?"

"If we are lucky, nothing, but whatever we find I will protect you. Have no fear."

They retired early, as they knew they were going to have a long day ahead of them. Draig was asleep in no time, but Drakeson was another story. The more he tried to go to sleep, the more he thought about Annwn. He had never been there, but he had heard stories. But in time, even Drakeson succumbed to sleep.

In the morning, Wilona prepared a large feast for them, as they would need to keep up their strength. With the feast over, Draig went out to the barn and harnessed the horse to the wagon. Then he went up into the loft and opened the chest. Pulling his sword from the chest, he strapped the sword to his side.

Coming out of the barn, Draig called for Drakeson. They climbed into the wagon and headed toward the Great Western Sea. Though they were in for long ride, they were in good spirits. Drakeson was excited at being a part of a legend.

When they reached the shore, Draig saw a small house and rode up to the door. He pulled a gold coin out of his pocket and offered it to the residence in exchange for them caring for the horse. The coin was quickly accepted, and the pair continued onto the beach.

"Now what do we do, Father?"

"We wait, my son, we just wait."

They stood on the beach and Drakeson looked out over the water. He saw a small patch of fog a short distance from the shore. As the fog neared the shore, Drakeson was finally able to pick out a shape in the middle.

When the shape got closer, the shape became more distinct. It was a small, flat-bottomed boat and the ferryman was tall and slender. He wore a black robe that reached to the floor and a hood that kept his face hidden in the shadows. He held a long pole with which he propelled the boat.

As the boat touched the shore, the ferryman motioned to them to come aboard. Once aboard, the ferryman pushed off and moved toward Annwn. At first, Drakeson just looked in the direction in which they travelled, hoping to catch a glimpse of the Isle of the Dead.

Finally, Drakeson got around to looking closer at the ferryman. But no matter how hard he tried, he could not see his face. He could see nothing but a dark shadow in the opening in the hood. When Drakeson looked down at the pole that the ferryman held, he had the shock of his life. His eyes locked on the ferryman's hands. They were bony skeletal hands.

Drakeson grabbed his father's arm, and said, "Look! Look!"

Draig interrupted, "Yes, I know."

That was all that Draig said and nothing more. It was obvious that it was only Drakeson who was caught by surprise as to whom or what the ferryman was. Drakeson did his best not to look directly at the ferryman the rest of the trip to the island.

As they approached the shore of Annwn, they found themselves in a thick fog. Drakeson was curious as to the fog that clung to the island.

"Father, how is it that the island is covered in fog?"

"The fog is but a shroud, an illusion that hides the island from the living."

When they stepped on the shore of Annwn, Drakeson looked around. He expected to see a thick fog blanketing the island, but it was clear and sunny. Drakeson then looked back to the ferryman, but he had vanished.

They made their way to where the portal spawns and began gathering wood to build a bonfire. Drakeson was surprised that there was so much wood just lying about on the ground. It seemed odd to Drakeson that the more wood they collected, the more wood there seemed to be.

They waited as the sun began to set on the horizon. At the first haze of dusk, Draig lit the bonfire as the portal slowly opened. It was only moments before the first spirits approached the open portal.

After a few moments, Drakeson heard a noise. It was a very soft noise at first, like that of a mosquito buzzing his ear, but then it grew louder until it was as loud as a whisper. It was then that he realized it was the sound of someone chanting in a low tone. He looked around for the source but saw nothing except the slow procession of spirits through the portal. He looked down to see that Draig's sword began to glow a soft green.

Drakeson asked, "Father, what is that?"

Draig drew his sword and held it up. He looked at Drakeson and grinned.

"Those who dwell within the Otherworld are spirits, so a physical weapon like my sword cannot harm them. The chanting you hear is in a language from the begin time. It phases my sword so that it is in both the physical world and the spirit world at the same time."

"Are you planning to go inside?" Drakeson asked.

"No, but you must realize that those inside can come out."

Drakeson took a step back. "They can come out here?"

"Do not worry, my son, if they do, I will take care of them in a most permanent way."

"Who is doing the chanting, Father?"

"Who else . . . the spirit of Draco."

Every now and then Drakeson could see a figure or two look out from the portal, but they would eventually move away. While they seemed curious with this side of the portal, they would not come out.

"Father, they look but do not come out?"

"Since time long forgotten, dragonriders have stood guard at this portal. They know and remember. This bonfire tells them there are many instead of one. It is easier to burn wood than to fight, is it not?"

"But, if they come through the portal?"

"They will not make that mistake a second time."

As the hours passed, Draig sat down to rest his eyes. Though his eyes were closed, he was not asleep. It was one of those times when the portal was quiet and nothing unusual was occurring. Drakeson continued to watch the portal while Draig rested.

He suddenly saw a woman step through the portal and walk toward him. She was fair skinned and had long flowing red hair. She wore a dress made of golden chainmail that came to just above the knee. She was carrying a golden shield and a long sword was strapped to her side. She also had a bow slung across her shoulder. Alarmed at her presence, Drakeson called out to his father:

"Father, Father, something is coming!"

Draig leaped to his feet with his glowing sword clinched tightly in his hand. He looked at the woman as she approached. Just steps away she stopped and simply stood there. She drew her sword and Draig held out his sword.

"Who bars this portal that keeps me from passing?"

"It is I, Draig, dragonrider!"

"Is that supposed to scare me?"

"Scared me the first time I heard it."

With that, they both burst out in laughter. Draig ran up to the woman and hugged her.

"Coinchend, it cannot be, but it is!"

"Hello, Draig, it has been a long time."

He put his arm on Drakeson's shoulder and said, "This is Drakeson, my son."

"I am a dragonrider, too," Drakeson said.

Coinchend bowed. "Drakeson, son of Draig, son of Anarcher, son of Eafa, I am honored to meet you."

Draig asked, "What brings you to this side of the portal?"

"I have come to visit the physical realm for a time." Coinchend said.

"Are you a spirit, Coinchend?" Drakeson asked.

"No, little one, I was human when I crossed through the portal to the Otherworld, but my body has long ago become accustomed to that realm. In this world I am like a fish out of water. I can only stay a short time, and then I must return to the realm of shadows."

"How long will you stay?" Drakeson asked.

"I must return to the Otherworld the next time that the portal opens, but I will stay here until that time."

"We would be honored if you stay with us, Coinchend," Draig offered. "I am sure that Drakeson would give up his room for such a special guest."

"I will give up my bed for our guest. I can sleep in the barn," Drakeson insisted.

"I am sure you can find a nice spot in the house to make a bed, my son."

They waited for the portal to close, and together they took the Bag on Noz across the water to the house and collected their horse and wagon. On the trip back to the farm, Coinchend and Draig exchanged stories. Drakeson hung on every word the pair said.

When they arrived at the farm, Wilona was standing in the doorway. Drakeson removed the harness from the horse and put him away while Draig introduced his guest.

"Wilona, I present to you Coinchend, warrior princess of the Otherworld! I told her she may stay in our home while she is on this side."

"We are honored to have you in our home," Wilona said.

"I am honored to meet the wife of Draig."

They sat down at the table, and Wilona brought them a large meal, a welcome offering for the weary travelers who had not eaten in so long. Coinchend sat there staring at her plate as if she did not know what she was supposed to do.

"Are you not hungry, Coinchend?" Drakeson asked.

"I have not known hunger for more years than I can remember."

"You do not eat in the Otherworld?" Drakeson asked.

"When I first arrived in the Otherworld, I felt hunger, so I would search for things to eat. But as the years passed, I forgot when it was that I no longer felt hunger or ate."

"Should we not eat in front of you?" Draig asked.

She reached down and picked up a small piece of meat and put it in her mouth. For a moment, the food just sat in her mouth, but then she began to chew. After a moment of savoring the food in her mouth, she swallowed.

"I forgot how much fun it was to eat!" Coinchend said with a smile.

"Eat, Coinchend, there is plenty enough to eat your fill!" Wilona said.

Coinchend began shoving food in her mouth as if she had not eaten in a fortnight. Then again, she had not eaten for a long time. Wilona thought that Coinchend would never get full, but it was good to see her eat so well.

After supper, Draig and Coinchend talked about great adventures. They talked about the past as if it were yesterday, exchanging stories until it was very late. As Wilona put her hand on his shoulder, he realized just how late it had become.

"Coinchend, you must be tired. Drakeson, clear your things from your room so that she may rest."

"Your son does not have to surrender his room to me. I can always sleep in the barn." Coinchend said.

"You are a guest in our home. We could not allow you to sleep in the barn," Wilona said.

Drakeson climbed the ladder to his room and brought down the things he needed and piled them in a corner of the room. Coinchend went up the ladder and went to sleep.

"How long is she here, my husband?"

"She will be here until the portal opens again. I hope you do not mind that I asked her to stay."

"No, my husband, you could do no less than to extend our hospitality to such an old friend."

"Thank you for your understanding, my wife," Draig said as he wandered into the bedroom to sleep.

As Wilona went about her evening chores, Drakeson made himself a bed on the floor in the living area. He sat there quietly watching his mother doing her chores. As he watched, he continued to think about Coinchend.

"I thought only men could be warriors," Drakeson said.

"What would make you think that?" asked Wilona.

"I have seen many soldiers at the hill forts, but I never saw a woman warrior."

"You have seen Coinchend, have you not?" Wilona asked.

"Yes, Mother."

"Does she not wear the clothes of a warrior?"

"Yes, Mother."

"Does she not carry a sword at her side?"

"Yes, Mother."

"Did your father not introduce her as Coinchend, warrior princess of the Otherworld?"

"Yes, Mother."

"Then why do you still question that fact?"

"I do not question the fact that she is a warrior. I simply said I thought only men could be warriors."

Wilona got a funny look on her face. She then went into the bedroom and went to bed. Draig lay down and thought about it some more.

"I simply asked," Drakeson said as he rolled over and went to sleep.

Chapter 6

"The Darkness Defeated"

Draig stepped out of the house in the early minutes before dawn. As he looked toward the barn, he saw something in the morning gloom. A dark form lay on the ground halfway between the house and the barn.

He was not sure what lay there in the dark. As he took a few steps forward, it became obvious that it was a man lying face down on the ground. Draig ran up to realize it was an Angeln hunter. His body was bloodied and motionless. Draig called out toward the house.

"Wilona, quick . . . bring water and cloth for bandages!"

Draig looked at the man's back and recognized that he had been severely flogged. He gently rolled the man over to see serious burns on his chest, as if a sword had been heated and placed against his flesh. He was not just beaten; he was tortured. Barely breathing, the man looked into Draig's eyes and managed to speak in a labored whisper.

"Great Cinaed, I have found you."

"Lie still. Rest . . . do not talk."

"They attacked us and he killed them. I escaped and came to you for help."

"Who killed them?"

"The evil one killed them, the draoidh. Great Cinaed, please make the pain go away."

At this time, Coinchend came rushing out of the door with her sword clutched in her hand. Wilona followed with a basin of water and scraps of cloth while Drakeson brought up the rear. The hunter gave out a great sigh, took his last breath and was gone.

"Nothing more to do. His pain is gone."

Draig reached down and closed the man's eyes. With tears running down his face he looked up at Drakeson and spoke in a soft voice:

"Drakeson, go and saddle the horse. It is time to take him home."

Drakeson ran into the barn as his father commanded. Coinchend moved closer to Draig and put a hand upon his shoulder. She looked at the tortured body of the man that lay motionless on the ground.

"Who is he?" Coinchend asked.

"He is an Angeln hunter. Their village is to the south."

"Where is the rest of his party?"

"They are waiting to enter the Otherworld."

"I understand, Draig, and I will look after them when they arrive in my realm," Coinchend said.

"We must return him to his village," Draig said, "and learn more about this draoidh who would do this thing to the Angeln."

Drakeson finished saddling and brought the horse out to where the man lay on the ground. Coinchend helped Draig gently lift the man up and laid him across the saddle as Drakeson held the horse still. As Draig began to lead the horse away, he turned back and called to Wilona:

"Wait inside the house until we return. Those who caused his death may come looking for him."

Wilona went into the house and bolted the door as the others began their trek south. The three trekkers were quiet and solemn as they continued their hike toward the village. They were not eager to have to tell the village that one of their hunters had died in such a horrible manner.

The trio stopped at the edge of the village, but at that point Draig continued to advance alone. As soon as the Angeln spotted Draig, they ran to him and fell to their knees.

"Great Cinaed, we are honored by your presence!"

"I bring bad tidings," Draig said. "I have found one of your hunters and brought him home."

Draig motioned to Drakeson to bring the horse forward. Coinchend remained at the edge of the village with her hand on her sword. As several men came and lowered the man from the horse, a woman fell to the ground wailing. It was obvious, even to Drakeson, that this was the hunter's wife. Other women gathered about her to comfort her while the men carried him away.

"And what of the others, Great Cinaed?" the elder asked.

"He was the only one who reached me," Draig explained.

The elder bowed his head and asked, "Who did this thing to our hunters?"

"He spoke of an evil one, a draoidh. Do you know of whom he spoke?"

The elder cleared his throat and said, "We have encountered a draoidh, but we turned him out because we belong to Cinaed. We have no need of him. But this draoidh—there is evil in his dark eyes."

"Does this draoidh have a name?" Draig asked.

"Yes, Great Cinaed, he is called Boda. They say he is the messenger of a powerful demon."

"And where would I find this Boda?"

"He is in the forest to the north of your circle of stones, Great Cinaed."

"I will have to look into this draoidh."

The elder then asked, "But can the others not be alive somewhere?"

Draig looked back toward Coinchend. She simply shook her head as she lowered her head in silence.

"Their voices have been silenced, and their spirits wait to cross into the Otherworld."

The elder looked past Draig to Coinchend. "Is this another of Cinaed's women?" he asked Draig.

Draig motioned to Coinchend and she walked up next to him. "This is Coinchend. She is Cinaed's voice in the Otherworld. This is why she knew the others have been silenced as well."

Draig's attention now turned to the fallen hunter. He had died in the presence of their god. He would now require something special, something befitting the stature of one who had died in the presence of his god.

"Bring wood that we can build a pyre," Draig commanded. "This hunter shall be afforded a funeral fit for a god!"

The Angeln collected wood and built a pyre in the center of the village. When it was prepared, they brought out the body of the hunter that they had wrapped in white cloth. They laid him on the pyre and backed away.

Draig brought his palms together and formed a ball of energy between his hands. The ball of energy became a fiery orb. He took the orb into his right hand and held it out in his open palm. As he let the orb grow bright, he called out what he had heard so many times before.

"From fire we are born, to fire we return. The body dies, but the spirit lives on. From fire we are born, to fire we return."

Hearing Draig speak it, the Angeln began chanting it over and over. Draig then blew on the orb, creating a large stream of flame that extended from the orb outward toward the pyre and setting it ablaze.

Draig motioned to Drakeson and Coinchend to back away while the Angeln were focusing on the pyre. Once at the edge of the village, they made haste to put distance between them and the Angeln.

"Why did we leave so abruptly?" asked Drakeson.

Draig came to a stop. "It is enough that they think I am their god. I remember Atumanus and how his actions with a tribe of people turned out. I do not wish to repeat his mistake. I do not want to influence the lives of the Angeln any more than absolutely necessary."

"What are we going to do about this Boda?" Coinchend asked.

"We are going to have to learn more about him and his followers before we can decide if we need to do anything."

"We have to decide if we have to do something?" Drakeson asked.

"We are dragonriders. Sometimes we are required to take action for the benefit of Man, and sometimes we have to simply let the world of Man alone."

"And how do we know which it is?"

Draig looked at Coinchend and smiled, saying, "A not so little bird will tell us."

Drakeson did not really understand what his father meant, but there were a lot of things that his father said that he did not really understand. Drakeson simply reckoned that he might figure it out as he got older.

When they arrived back at the farm, Draig went into the house and gathered some food before getting his bow. Coming out of the house, Draig called to Coinchend:

"I think we need to do some hunting. I will get my sword."

"Shall I get my bow, too, Father?" Drakeson asked.

"No, my son, this is a different kind of hunting. We are going to be hunting a very dangerous kind of animal. This is an animal you are better off not learning to hunt because it is very difficult to quit once you begin."

Coinchend went into the house and got her bow while Draig got his sword from the loft. Next, Draig hooked the wagon to the horse. Drakeson stood at the door feeling hurt, but he understood that his father knew what was best for him. Draig strapped his sword to his side and called out to Wilona as he climbed into the wagon.

"We will be back before supper if things go as planned."

"What if things do not go as planned?" Wilona called after them.

Draig did not answer as they headed off toward the circle of stones. He obviously did not want to acknowledge that there was even the slightest possibility that things would go awry.

When they arrived at the circle of stones, there was someone standing in the center of the stones and looking toward the forest to the north. He was a tall and slender man with a long, flowing beard and hair that had long turned gray. He also carried a staff with a polished quartz crystal embedded at the crown. He wore a dark blue robe fastened at the waist with a gold braided rope, which ends reached to his knees.

"Hello, old friend," Draig called out as he stepped down from the wagon.

"Good day, Draig," said Myrddin without turning around.

"What brings you here, my friend?"

"I felt ripples in the treoir and they drew me here."

"What do you sense, Myrddin?" Coinchend asked.

"I sense a hunger that goes unfed, an ancient evil that never dies. I feel it, but I cannot see it. I sense that it does not want me to see it."

"Do you see anything else?" Draig asked.

"I see others coming," Myrddin said. "Our circle grows larger. I can see them approaching, but they are still far away."

"It is time we begin our hunt," Draig said. "It will not be an easy task, and the day is slipping away as we speak."

"I will stay here and wait for your return," Myrddin said, "and do my best to cut through the fog that limits my vision."

Myrddin climbed into the back of the wagon and sat down as Draig and Coinchend turned north and headed into the forest. There was no question why Myrddin remained behind. They knew there was more than one way to get the information they sought, and he was simply trying one of the other ways.

They moved through the forest for a couple hours when they heard the clumsy footsteps of the animal Man. They crouched in the bushes and spied four men in black, hooded robes. On closer inspection, Draig and Coinchend could detect the presence of swords beneath their robes. They looked at each other and nodded. These men were followers of Boda.

Draig and Coinchend slowly drew their swords and looked at each other. With a nod and a wink, they charged out of the bushes with swords waving in the air and both screaming like banshees.

The four men were so stunned and surprised by the two warriors coming out of the bushes that they fumbled their swords trying to get them out from under their robes. Draig and Coinchend closed in, and the men quickly dropped their swords.

Draig turned to Coinchend and said, "This was way too easy."

Draig reached down and picked up one of the swords and tossed it back to one of the followers. The man caught the sword by the hilt and looked at Draig and then looked to his companions. He charged Draig, but Draig easily disarmed him.

"Come on, you can't do better than that?" Draig taunted the man.

Draig picked up the sword and tossed it back to the man again. Again, Draig easily disarmed him. The third time Draig tossed the man the sword, but he refused to pick it up.

Coinchend said, "Why do you bother? You already know he is no match for you."

Draig turned to the man and said, "I apologize. My behavior was unbecoming a warrior as myself."

Draig and Coinchend tied each man to a tree with a length of rope, and then Draig began to question them about Boda. The men would not speak. They just stared off into the distance as he asked them questions. It was obvious to Draig that he was not going to get any answers.

Coinchend turned to Draig. "Interrogation is not in a dragon's job description. Perhaps you would be more useful if you scouted back toward the circle to make sure we are still alone."

"What are you saying?" asked Draig.

"Take a walk, dragon. Trust me when I say you do not want to be here right now."

Draig gave Coinchend a puzzled look and then looked at the men tied to the trees. He did not know what Coinchend had in mind, but nothing he was doing was going to work. He slowly backed up a few steps at a time. Each time he stopped, he looked at the men and saw fear in their eyes. Finally, Draig turned around and walked away.

Coinchend watched as Draig disappeared into the trees and then turned her attention to the prisoners. She walked up to the first man and knelt before him. She then motioned to where Draig had gone.

"He is dragon. He is bound by an ancient oath of honor, but I am not. I am going to ask you questions and you are going to answer. If you do not, the events that transpire are of your own making."

The man looked at Coinchend. He grinned in defiance and then stared off into the distance. It was obvious that he was not going to willingly cooperate. Coinchend leaned in close and turned the man's head so that he had to look at her.

"There are things in the Otherworld more horrible than you can imagine. Look into my eyes and witness one of the horrors."

At first, the man resisted, but in the end he could not fight her. He gazed into her eyes and his gaze became fixed. He was unable to move or look away, locked into a trance from which he could not break free. As he looked into her eyes he saw shadows approaching.

"They are the Cwn Annwn, the hounds of death. Hear them howl as they rend your flesh."

The man's eyes became wild. His heart pounded in his chest as he squirmed in vain to break his bonds. He finally let out a blood curdling scream, and then there was silence. She loosed the ropes from the man's wrists and let him slump to the ground. Coinchend rose and looked to the other three men.

"He should have just told me what I wanted to know. I will have to explain that to him in the Otherworld when I see him. Okay, who wishes to be next?"

She moved on to her next victim and repeated the process. Each man saw his own version of horror, but the results were much the same.

Meanwhile, after about an hour of wandering around a short distance away, Draig decided it was time to go back and see how Coinchend was getting along in her interrogations. When he got back, she was sitting on a rock and polishing her sword.

He looked at the men as they lay motionless on the ground. When he looked closely into their faces, he saw grotesque, disfigured faces looking back at him. It took only a moment for Draig to realize that they had been literally scared to death.

"And so it begins," Draig thought out loud. "Did you get anything from them?" he asked Coinchend.

"Not as much as I had hoped," Coinchend said. "Each one became a bit more cooperative than the one before him after having watched me interrogate the others. Boda is not a true draoidh. He is the servant of some powerful demon, but none of the four were aware of its name. Boda calls himself the messenger of the Saetan."

"It is not so unusual for a demon to protect its name, but it would be helpful to know what we are dealing with," Draig said.

"So, what do we do now?" Coinchend asked.

"For now, we return to Myrddin at the circle of stones. It is getting late, so we go home, and perhaps tomorrow we will find Boda and learn who this Saetan is."

Pointing at the four men, Draig asked, "And what about them?"

"We leave them as they are. They will serve as a warning to Boda that something is hunting him."

They returned to the circle of stones. Once reunited with Myrddin they explained what they had learned from the captured followers.

Myrddin then explained about the Saetan: "Saetan comes from a begin time language. He is a prophecy that is supposed to bring a thousand years of chaos. Not much remains of the language, so only part of the prophecy remains."

"Where could Boda have learned of the Saetan?" Coinchend asked.

"It is a very old legend, but perhaps it has survived in some form or another."

Since there was little else to say about the Saetan until they learned more, they talked about old times while they rode back to the farm. As they approached the farm, Draig noticed two figures sitting on the stone bench by the oak tree. Draig quickly recognized them, jumping down from the wagon and running to them.

"Thibalexis, my old friend, what brings you here?"

"A not so little bird whispered in my ear and here I am."

"And you, Captain Arimah, how did you happen to come?"

"Thibalexis booked passage on my ship. As we ate supper, he mentioned that he was coming to help an old friend. When I noticed his sword, I knew I had only seen one like it in all my life. It was no surprise to me that he was speaking of my friend, Draig. I could not resist volunteering my services, such as they are."

"What about your ship?"

"What about it? My crew is the best crew in the world. They will continue to sail back and forth between here and Marseille until I return. Thibalexis did not say, but I assume I am returning?"

"I make no promises, but my plan is that we all go home when this is over."

They sat there talking for most of an hour as Drakeson and Wilona watched from the doorway. They did not want to get in the way of such a warm reunion. After all, there would be plenty of time for them to take part later.

"Come, let us eat," Draig said, "and then we can decide what course we shall take next."

Pausing at the door, he said, "This is my wife, Wilona, and my son, Drakeson."

Turning to his family, he said, "You already know Myrddin and Coinchend. These are my friends Thibalexis and Captain Arimah."

Drakeson asked, "Are you dragonriders too?"

"Yes, Drakeson, I am a dragonrider like your father," Thibalexis replied.

Captain Arimah said, "I am but a simple ship captain, but I am beginning to see that there is something I should know more about."

Draig said, "Yes, perhaps it is time you learn more about your passengers, but for now let us eat.

They went into the house and Wilona began preparing supper while Drakeson put the wagon away and unharnessed the horse. Drakeson would rather have been in the house with the others, but someone had to care of the horse. When Drakeson finished, he headed back to the house.

Thibalexis asked, "What are our plans for tomorrow?"

Draig let out a sigh. "I guess our priority tomorrow needs to be hunting and gathering more food. There are now many mouths to feed and not enough food to feed them all."

"We have enough people to divide into two groups, one for hunting and one for gathering," said Coinchend.

Coming in the door, Drakeson chimed in, "I will go hunting with you, Coinchend!"

"Yes, Drakeson, my littlest friend," Coinchend said with a smile, "it will be my great honor to hunt with you!"

As they sat down to eat, Captain Arimah added, "I would like to join you also, though I have not hunted for a long time. There is simply very little prey running around the deck of a ship."

Myrddin quipped, "I guess we know who the gatherers are."

"It is okay, Myrddin," Draig said laughingly, "even the mighty have to be a gatherer at times."

"And what will we do after that?" Captain Arimah then asked.

"That is what I hope to find out after supper," Draig said.

During supper, the conversation turned to more pleasurable topics. They exchanged stories about what they had done since they last met up together. Once supper concluded, Draig picked up his wine bottle and headed out the door to the barn. The others stood up and looked at each other as if to ask what they should do.

Wilona said, "Please, remain here and rest. This is his normal ritual. He goes out to the barn every night."

"Why does he do that?" asked Captain Arimah.

"To honor friends long since gone," Wilona responded.

"Leave him to his traditions," Myrddin added. "We will wait here until he returns."

Draig climbed the stairs to the loft and picked up the cup that sat behind the chest. He filled the cup with wine and placed the bottle on the floor. Draig knelt on the floor and held up his cup.

"Bellorus, old friend, I drink to your memory!" And he took a sip from his cup.

"Dormanus, old friend, I drink to your memory!" And he took a sip from his cup.

"Melkoran, old friend, I drink to your memory!" And he took a sip from his cup.

Draig placed his cup on top of the chest, but instead of descending the stairs he simply stood there facing the wall. He did not move for several minutes, and then he called out:

"Spirit of Draco, it is time that we have a talk, do you not agree?"

He stood there for a few minutes without an answer to his question. And then it began to grow brighter in the loft, and then there came a familiar voice from behind him. Draig turned around to find the spirit of a dragon standing in the loft.

"You have called out to me and I have come."

"I seek your help, spirit of Draco, as I have questions to which I require answers."

"Ask your questions, Draig, and I will enlighten you as best as I am able."

"Tell me of the Saetan, spirit of Draco."

"The Saetan was one of the Great Ones of your ancestors. He was from the begin time, long before Man walked upon the earth. He used his magic for dark purposes. For that reason he was slowly pulled into darkness and became lost in the shadows. As time passed, darkness consumed him and he became a powerful daemon."

"What became of the Saetan?"

"As the Saetan's power grew, he became too dangerous to allow him to go unchecked. As the ruler dragons combined their magic to hold him in place, Tiamat and the other dragons caused a portal to open to another dimension. The ruler dragons then pushed the Saetan through the portal, closing the portal and sealing him inside."

"What does this draoidh, Boda, have to do with the Saetan?"

"I do not know who this Boda is. I only know that there is a prophecy. The prophecy says the Saetan will escape his prison and bring a thousand years of darkness, and chaos shall envelope the world."

"Is there anything more, spirit of Draco?"

"There is no more that I can tell you, dragon," said the spirit of Draco.

"Thank you, spirit of Draco."

As Draig stood there, the loft dimmed as quickly as it had grown bright and the dragon spirit faded. Draig turned back toward the chest, picked up his cup and drank the last of his wine. He placed the cup in its place behind the chest, picked up the wine bottle and returned to the house.

As Draig opened the door and came into the house, the others were sitting there anxiously waiting for him. Draig put the bottle back on the shelf and sat quietly in his chair. The others tried to be patient, but patience has its limits.

Thibalexis asked, "What have you learned?"

"We have to find Boda and find out what he is up to," Draig said.

"Can we please get beyond the obvious?" Myrddin said.

Draig cleared his throat. "A prophecy says the Saetan will escape his prison and bring a thousand years of darkness, and Chaos shall envelope the world."

Coinchend asked, "And this Boda is the key to the prophecy?"

"I do not know," said Draig. "I assume we will find that out when we find him. As for now, we have a long day ahead of us, so I suggest we get some sleep."

Myrddin, Thibalexis and Captain Arimah elected to sleep in the barn since the house had limited room for guests. Thinking that this was more of a camping trip than simple sleeping arrangements, Drakeson chose to sleep in the barn with them. They pulled up some hay to make their beds, though sleep did not come quickly.

"When are we going to discuss what is going on?" Captain Arimah asked.

"We are all dragonriders!" Drakeson shouted.

Thibalexis jumped into the conversation. "We were born sons of Man, but we have lived out our lives among dragons."

"Dragons are not real!" Captain Arimah demanded.

Drakeson, mimicking his father, said, "They are as real as you and I, my son, and I was honored to walk among them. Alas, they no longer walk among us."

Myrddin chuckled and said, "Our young friend has learned well, perhaps too well. Thibalexis, Draig, and I have soared above the clouds on the wings of dragons. We have stood beside them and fought for truth and honor."

"Surely, dragons are but stories spoken under one's breath," Captain Arimah said.

"Dragons are as real as the sun that rises in the morning and the moon that shines at night," Drakeson said.

Thibalexis added, "Once there were many, but now there are none. They have left Man to his own fate but for those few of us, the dragonriders, who remain in the shadows to protect Man from himself."

"Does Man need protection?" Captain Arimah asked.

"Do we not now stand before the precipice?" Myrddin asked. "Do you not feel the breath of Fate on the back of our necks? Even now I sense something watches us from the shadows."

"Perhaps it is the Angeln," Drakeson said. "They often watch us from just beyond the trees."

"We can only hope that is all it is," Myrddin said as he rolled over and closed his eyes.

The others followed close behind, knowing they had a busy day ahead of them. Those in the house had already retired in preparation for the coming day, knowing the sun rises early.

They awoke just before dawn. Coinchend, Drakeson, and Captain Arimah headed off with bows to hunt some game while the others began gathering other items. The hunting party had little trouble locating and bringing down a red deer, while the gathering group brought home wild carrots, crabapples and an assortment of nuts.

They put away the fruit and nuts they gathered. They slaughtered the red deer and tanned the hide for use later. They also prepared the antlers as a trophy for Captain Arimah to hang in his cabin on his ship. They used the rest of the day to rest and prepare for what would come in the morning.

As the sun rose the next morning, everyone woke to an early meal. They ate heartily, as they knew it could be their only meal of the day. This small army of friends then gathered their swords and their bows. As they were about to leave, Drakeson called out:

"I shall get my weapons too!"

Draig took him by the shoulder, "No, my son, your place is here with your mother."

"But I want to help. Am I not a warrior too?"

"Sometimes, warriors have to protect those that are left behind," Draig explained. "Who would protect your mother if you were to go with us?"

"It is not fair!" Drakeson demanded.

"When you grow older, you will find that the world is rarely fair," Myrddin responded.

Drakeson sat down and pouted, but he knew that the others were right. Someone had to remain behind to protect his mother, and that meant it was going to be him.

When they walked out of the house, they found four white stallions waiting for them outside. Draig was not surprised in the least. He simply ran past them and into the barn to saddle his horse. The others, on the other hand, were extremely surprised.

Captain Arimah asked, "Where did these magnificent horses come from?"

Myrddin explained. "I summoned them from Sidhe, home of the faeries. They are the four horses of the faerie Apocalis the Hunter. There is a prophecy that the four horses of Apocalis will carry heroes who shall save the world!"

Captain Arimah asked, "Faeries are real as well?"

"As real as these horses," Myrddin answered. "If the faerie Apocalis did not exist, how could the four horses of Apocalis exist?"

"Tell us more about this prophecy," asked Captain Arimah. "It just might keep us alive!"

"It is only a prophecy, and I do not pay much attention to prophecies," Myrddin said with a laugh. "Then again, since it is always a possibility that the prophecy is real, are you not glad that I brought them?"

"Would it not be greatly rewarding to be the heroes who save the world?" Coinchend asked.

"Only if we live to enjoy it!" Captain Arimah quipped.

Thibalexis spoke up. "Is there a greater honor than to die saving the world?"

"I would rather live saving the world than to die saving the world," Captain Arimah said. "Is there not room for both?"

Just then, Draig brought his horse out of the barn, and the little army mounted and rode toward the northern forest. They were in good cheer on this part of the journey, but there was an underlying sense that things could go badly very quickly.

As they entered the forest, they still had many unanswered questions, but they were not going to leave the forest until they had those answers. They did not know who Boda was or where to find him. They did not know how many followers he had or how many of his followers would be with him when they found him. Regardless, it was imperative that they find him and find him quickly.

After a few hours of searching, they happened upon a patrol of Boda's followers in their black, hooded robes. The six men were walking a well-worn path. Draig looked at the others and then shouted:

"Take them alive!"

They swooped in on them like ants to a lump of sugar. The followers attempted to put up a fight, but they were no match for dragonriders. Even Captain Arimah showed them how capable a warrior a Phoenician ship captain could be. After only a few minutes the followers were disarmed and tied to trees.

After attempting to interrogate them for a few minutes, it became obvious they were not going to divulge anything useful. Draig did not like the option, but there was little choice in the matter.

"Thibalexis and Myrddin, you ride south and see that the path is clear. Captain Arimah and I will ride east and see that the path is clear in that direction."

Captain Arimah asked, "And what about these prisoners?"

"Do not worry," Coinchend said, "I can handle them."

The men mounted and rode off in both directions. Coinchend watched Draig and the others until they disappeared into the distance and then turned her attention to the prisoners. She walked up to the first man and knelt before him.

"They are dragons. They are bound by an ancient oath, but I am not. I am going to ask you questions and you are going to answer. If you do not, the events that transpire are of your own making."

The man looked at Coinchend. As she asked questions he remained silent. It was obvious that he was not going to willingly cooperate. Coinchend leaned in real close and turned his head so that he had to look at her.

"There are things in the Otherworld more horrible than you can imagine. Look into my eyes and witness one of the horrors."

At first, the man resisted, but in the end he could not resist. He gazed into her eyes and his gaze became fixed. He was unable to move or look away. He was locked into a trance and he could not break free. As he looked into her eyes he saw shadows approaching.

"They are the Cwn Annwn, the hounds of death. Hear them howl as they rend your flesh."

The man's eyes flinched wildly. His heart pounded in his chest as he squirmed trying to break his bonds. He finally let out a blood curdling scream, and then there was silence. Finally, she loosed the ropes from the man's wrists and let him slump to the ground. Coinchend then rose and looked to the other five men.

"He should have just told me what I wanted to know. I will have to explain that to him when I see him in the Otherworld. All right, who wishes to be next?"

She moved on to her next victim and repeated the process. By the time Draig and the others returned, Coinchend was sitting on a rock. As they looked around, five of the followers were lying motionless on the ground. The sixth was leaning against a tree. He was wild-eyed and trembling and was mumbling to himself.

Captain Arimah was the first to speak up. "What in the name of Baal has happened here?"

"They refused to answer my questions. It was their choice, not mine," Coinchend said.

Pointing at the sixth follower, Thibalexis asked, "And what about that one?"

Coinchend answered, "He is lost within his own mind. He will either remain there or he will not."

Myrddin reached into his pouch and pulled out a short length of bamboo, both ends plugged with wax. As soon as he removed the wax from one end, a most horrible odor filled the air.

"Oh my! Whatever crawled in there and died?" Captain Arimah said.

Myrddin smiled as he pulled a strange, unknown leaf from inside the bamboo and placed it in the man's mouth. At first there was no change, but soon the man stopped trembling and no longer mumbled. He was now sitting quietly and staring off into the distance.

Myrddin spoke to the man: "Listen to my words and belief. You no longer follow Boda. You feel a desire to return home. Go now, go home."

The man slowly rose and began walking south along the road. Myrddin put the wax back into the end of the bamboo and put it back into his pouch. The others watched as the man slowly continued south until he disappeared in the distance.

"What was that?" asked Thibalexis.

"It is a secret that has existed since the begin time," Myrddin explained. "He will wake today, tomorrow, perhaps the day after."

"Then what?" Captain Arimah asked. "Will he return to Boda and warn him?"

"He may remember who he is and attempt to return," Myrddin explained, "but it is also more likely he will remember what occurred here and decide to get as far away from here as possible. But then, he may remember nothing and simply return home."

Coinchend asked, "How long before he can remember who he is and return to Boda?"

"I would say no sooner than tomorrow," Myrddin said. "His mind was severely troubled. It will take a long time for the fog to clear from his mind."

Coinchend said, "The man told me much before he hid within his own mind. There is a shack a few leagues ahead on this road. Boda might be within, but he will be guarded."

"Quickly, to your horses!" Draig commanded. "We will reach Boda long before the man can return."

They mounted and road north. The farther they rode, the more they quickened their pace. They found themselves driven by a force they could not resist, nor would they if they could. Finally, they came across a small shack hidden in a clump of trees just off the road.

They hid their horses at a safe distance and crept up to the small shack. As they got closer, they saw five of Boda's followers standing around outside. Being careful to avoid alerting the guards, they crouched in the bushes and watched. There was no activity around the shack other than the guards outside. They could not help but wonder if Boda was inside.

Captain Arimah whispered, "If we each choose a target, we can drop all of them without them being able to give an alarm to anyone inside."

Draig whispered, "And so it begins."

"Is there a problem?" Captain Arimah asked.

"It is the first law that bothers them," Coinchend answered. "Take no action whose intent brings harm to others. It is a law they take very seriously. Once you kill, it does not get harder; it gets easier."

"We realize that we have no choice but to kill," Draig explained. "That does not mean we take killing lightly. Is it so strange that as warriors we spend so many years learning to kill so that we can try so hard not to kill?"

"So let us get this over with," Myrddin added. "All we are doing is postponing the inevitable."

Each of them selected their target and cocked an arrow. All at once they let their arrows fly, and all five of the guards dropped to the ground. They drew their swords and charged the shack.

Once inside, they discovered that there appeared to be no one in the shack. The shack was dimly lit by sunlight that broke through cracks in the roof. The shack was sparsely furnished with a large table in the center and a few chairs scattered around the perimeter of the room.

On the table were a large tome and four black candles, one set at each corner of the table. As Draig approached the book, he saw that the front of the book was covered in dark runes. As Draig ran his hand across the front of the book, he spoke the runes aloud:

"Ta tiem deshne. Ta tiem ovrai deim deshne."

Thibalexis asked, "What did you say? What does this mean?"

"There is no exact translation. Basically, it says the time grows near. The time grows nearer every day."

"Time grows near for what?" Captain Arimah asked.

"It is a tome," Draig explained, "a grimoire—a book of incantations and summoning spells."

Draig then noticed the red ribbon that was the bookmarker. Hesitantly, he closed his eyes and slowly opened the book to the page that was marked. Draig then opened his eyes and scanned the page. He became noticeably pale, and his hand began to tremble as he moved his fingers across the incantation written on the page.

"It cannot be! Even he cannot be contemplating such a thing!"

"So tell us," said Captain Arimah, "what is it that it says? What—"

Myrddin interrupted. "It is a summoning spell. But it is not just any summoning spell. It is a summoning spell for the Saetan, the Dark One."

"You said he was imprisoned forever!" demanded Captain Arimah.

Draig cleared his voice and spoke: "The Great Ones believe in redemption. Because there was even the slightest chance for the Saetan to atone for his past, a spell was created to allow the portal to be reopened and thus the Saetan would be released from his prison."

" And the prison would require a great deal of energy to open the portal," Myrddin added.

Thibalexis asked, "But where would they find a source of energy great enough to…"

"The circle of stone!" they all answered at once.

"Come, we must stop them before they destroy the world!" Draig shouted as he bolted from the shack.

They ran for their horses and rode hard toward the circle of stones. Their hearts pounded in their chests with anticipation as they rode through the trees. They drew their swords as they broke through the tree line and began to ride across the open plain.

As Draig and his small army closed ground, Boda and his followers were already gathered at the circle of stones. They were dancing, jumping up and down, and screaming wildly. Boda looked up and noticed Draig and his companions bearing down on them.

Boda pointed toward them and exclaimed: "The four horses of Apocalis approach! They must not fulfill the prophecy! Kill them! Kill them all!"

Boda remained at the circle as his followers quickly drew their weapons and ran off to meet Draig's small party. They were not very well trained, but they made up for it with their numbers.

As Draig's small army closed the distance on their mounts, they saw before them a sea of flesh and steel that stood between them and the circle of stones. They rode full charge and crashed into the front of the massive army of followers. Just then, they heard voices from behind Boda's followers.

"Fight for Cinaed! Fight to the death!"

Fear and confusion filled the hearts of Boda's followers. As they crashed into Draig and his companions, the Angeln warriors pushed them from behind. Though Boda's army still outnumbered their enemies, they felt whirling swords hacking away on two fronts now.

Hearing the approach of heavy horses, Draig looked to the east and saw a dozen Roman soldiers charging with their swords drawn. Draig could only hope the Romans were there to help and not to hinder. It was now time to bring this all to a swift end.

"Deal with them," Draig yelled, "and I will deal with Boda personally!"

While the others continued the fight with the followers, Draig climbed onto one of the white stallions and rode toward the circle of stones. As Draig approached the circle, the ground shook and the stones began to glow a soft blue. Draig realized that Boda had already begun the spell when lightning rose from the stones and reached up into the sky.

Draig jumped down from the horse and ran toward Boda. It was then that the draoidh turned and struck out at Draig with his staff. Draig dropped to his knees and slid toward Boda as the staff passed over his head. From his kneeling position, Draig thrust his sword upwards with both hands, piercing Boda's body. Draig then gave his sword a twist. The feel of warm blood ran down Draig's arms and the draoidh's body slumped forward.

As Boda lay dead on the ground at his feet, Draig looked up and realized that he was too late, that Boda had already finished the spell, and the portal was beginning to open.

It would be only a matter of seconds before the portal would be open wide enough for the Saetan to pass through. Draig picked up the draoidh's staff and orb. With the end of the staff, he quickly drew a pentagram on the ground and stepped into it.

Tapping his staff three times at the north side of the pentagram, he spoke:

"Lugnasa, ruler of the northern dragons, I summon thee!" He held up the orb. "Grant me the power of your magic!" And the orb grew bright.

Tapping his staff three times at the east side of the pentagram, he spoke again:

"Beltaine, ruler of the eastern dragons, I summon thee!" He held up the orb. "Grant me the power of your magic!" And the orb grew brighter.

Tapping his staff three times at the south side of the pentagram, he spoke again:

"Imbolic, ruler of the southern dragons, I summon thee!" He held up the orb. "Grant me the power of your magic!" And the orb grew brighter still.

Tapping his staff three times at the west side of the pentagram he spoke once more:

"Samhain, ruler of the western dragons, I summon thee!" He held up the orb. "Grant me the power of your magic!" And the orb grew brighter.

Draig saw a shadow moving beyond the portal. As the daemon approached, Draig recognized that the Saetan was not a daemon. He was instead a great black dragon.

Draig held out the orb and spoke: "I, Draig, forbid you to enter this world!"

The Saetan Reached out from the other dimension and grabbed Draig about the throat and stepped into this world. He laughed, and then anger came to his deep red eyes.

"How dare a mere human command the Lord of Eternal Darkness!"

Suddenly, a great beam of white light projected from the orb, and the dragon broke his hold on Draig's throat.

Draig was finally able to speak: "I was once son of Man," Draig proclaimed, "but I became Draig, dragonrider. And now I am dragon!"

By now, Boda's followers had broken ranks and began to run toward the safety of the forest. The Angeln and the Romans ran after them. The others grabbed their horses and rode toward the circle of stones to assist Draig.

The Saetan recovered momentarily and moved toward Draig once more. As he reached out to Draig, Draig took a step backwards, and once again Draig held out the orb.

"In the begin time you were banished from this world. And now, in the name of Tiamat, I banish you once more!"

The orb once again grew bright, and the power of the light blinded the Saetan so that he could not see to strike out at Draig.

Draig invoked the words: "Mi fogair sibh! Mi fogair sibh air uile suthainneachd!"

The Saetan yelled, "No! I will not go back!"

"I banish you! I exile you to your prison for all eternity!"

As the power of the light grew brighter, the dragon stumbled backward, unable to resist. Unable to fight the light, the dragon stepped back through the portal and hid in the shadows beyond.

"By the power of the Light I command this portal to close!" Draig commanded.

Draig tossed the orb toward the portal. Clouds formed above the portal, and bolts of lightning reached down from the sky and struck the portal. The portal slowly closed, sealing the Saetan back into his prison in the other dimension.

With the draoidh dead and the Saetan safely sealed in his prison, Draig fell to the ground, weak and drained. It was then that Draig's comrades reached his side.

Draig whispered, "Quick, retrieve the tome and bring it here."

Thibalexis and Captain Arimah mounted their horses and rode hard to get to the book while the others tended to Draig. Once they arrived at the shack, Thibalexis wrapped the book in his cloak, and they returned to the circle of stones.

With the book safely in their possession, they laid the book on a large stone in the center of the circle of stones.

Draig motioned to Myrddin and whispered in his ear: "Destroy it. Destroy it now, so that it can never be used again."

Myrddin brought his palms together and drew in the treoir. The treoir became a fiery orb. Myrddin held up the fiery orb and let it grow bright. Myrddin threw down the orb onto the book, and with a blinding flash of light the book burst into flames. The flames changed colors from red to blue to green as the book was consumed. Soon there was nothing but ashes remaining where the book had once rested.

With the Saetan sealed back inside his dimension and the book forever consumed, Coinchend and Captain Arimah helped Draig onto his saddle and took him back to the farm to rest.

Myrddin and Thibalexis collected the ashes of the book and placed them in a small silk pouch. Myrddin again brought his palms together and drew in the treoir. The treoir became a swirling orb.

Myrddin held out the orb, and the air began to rotate around the large stone in the center of the circle. Slowly the stone began to rise into the air. At first it was but inches high, but in seconds it hovered two feet above the ground.

Thibalexis then dug a small hole in the ground where the stone had rested and placed the silk pouch into the hole. He then covered it over with dirt. Slowly the swirling air began to dissipate and the large stone lowered to the ground. With even the ashes now inaccessible, Thibalexis and Myrddin returned to the farm to see to Draig.

Chapter 7

"Returned to the Fold"

Draig was still weak and drained when they got back to the farm. Captain Arimah and Coinchend helped him down from his horse and into bed. They then joined the others to watch Myrddin dismiss the four horses of Apocalis.

"Ceithir eachs bho Apocalis!" Myrddin began. "An cein sibh thig, gu cein sibh rach air ais! Return from whence you came!"

The horses reared their heads several times and whinnied. Slowly they began to sparkle as if the stars in the sky were twinkling around them. They then began to fade a little at a time until they faded away altogether, vanishing into thin air.

Myrddin, Captain Arimah, Thibalexis, and Coinchend all came back into the house after the horses of Apocalis were returned to Sidhe. Wilona prepared them a hearty meal, after which they rested from the day's trials. She then went in to see Draig and tried to feed him a broth. He did not take it well, but he did swallow a good portion of it.

As it was a long day, the men soon wandered off to the barn, and Coinchend made her way up the ladder to Drakeson's room to sleep. But Drakeson did not go to the barn with the men. Instead, he stayed in the main room so as to be close to his ailing father.

In the morning, Myrddin went in to check on Draig, who was feeling better than the night before but was still a little weak. Myrddin had Wilona make Draig a bowl of stew, and before she took it in to Draig, Myrddin sprinkled some powder into it and stirred it to hide the powder.

Myrddin then decided it was time to turn his attention to other things. He bid his companions farewell and headed west. The others watched him as he walked off into the distance. He grew smaller as he got further away and eventually disappeared into the distance. The others decided to remain at the farm for a few more days of rest and to reminisce before going their separate ways.

The following day, Draig got up and attempted to do his chores. Drakeson ran along behind him to help him. Just the same, it took him much longer than normal, but at least they got it done. When Draig was finished with the chores, he went into his room and went to bed.

The next day, Draig got up and tried to do his chores again, but he was having little success. The harder he tried, the harder it was for him to focus on his chores. He was also becoming restless and unable to relax. Every time he sat down and tried to get comfortable, he felt the urge to get up and do something. He would never actually accomplish anything, for as soon as he would begin he would feel the need to quit and sit down.

Since Draig was not doing very well, his friends decided to remain at the farm until Draig got better. As the days passed it was becoming obvious that he was not getting better; he was getting worse.

Draig would try to sleep, but his sleep was filled with dark dreams. Unable to sleep any significant length of time, dark circles formed around his eyes, and his appetite was minimal at best.

Finally, the morning came when Draig did not get out of bed. Wilona went in to find his body consumed with fever and covered with sweat. She had Drakeson run to the river to fetch cold water, and she used the water to make cold compresses to lower the fever.

After a couple of days, Draig took a turn for the worse. He began spending increasingly longer periods in a delirious state with shorter waking hours in between. His waking hours were becoming shorter with every passing day.

As the days passed, Draig grew weaker. Wilona and Drakeson stood vigil over him, but still his health continued to get worse. Finally, the day came when he refused to eat at all. Try as they may, there was nothing they could do to improve his condition.

One day there was a knock on the front door, and when they opened the door they were surprised to see Myrddin standing there. Without saying a word, he came into the house and went straight to Draig's side. Myrddin rubbed herbs on Draig's chest and forehead. He made him eat strange looking leaves. For two days he labored over Draig, using every herb he had in his bag of medicinal herbs, but it was to no avail.

Finally, Myrddin came out of the room and sat down. At first, he simply stared at the floor. The others gathered around him, fearing the news was not going to be good.

Speaking in a whisper, Myrddin said, "I have tried everything that Belenus taught me about healing, but nothing has slowed his illness. There is nothing more I can do for him. None of my herbs can remove the curse of darkness."

Captain Arimah asked, "I do not understand. What is this curse of darkness?"

Myrddin started to explain. "It begins with but a touch, but it rapidly spreads, and—"

Wilona interrupted him. "What is spreading? What is happening to my husband?"

"The darkness is an evil from the begin time and is a force that is all consuming," Myrddin continued to explain. "When Draig confronted the Saetan, the Saetan reached out and touched him. I have done my best to help him. While I have managed to slow the darkness, nothing can stop the spread. Therefore, as the darkness grows within him, his ability to resist it wanes."

Thibalexis interjected, "Come out with it. What are you trying not to tell us?"

Myrddin interrupted him, saying, "Draig's time draws near. I am afraid that he will not see tomorrow. We must take him to the circle of stones."

Captain Arimah asked, "Why do we have to go there?"

"Because that is where dragons go to die," Coinchend said softly.

Captain Arimah asked, "What are you talking about? What do dragons have to do with Draig?"

Myrddin put his hand on Captain Arimah's shoulder and said, "You will understand . . . sooner than you think."

As evening approached, Myrddin sent Drakeson to the loft to fetch Draig's armor and sword. While Drakeson helped Myrddin put the armor on Draig, Thibalexis and Captain Arimah went out to the barn to hook the horse to the wagon.

While Drakeson and Myrddin finished making Draig look presentable, Coinchend went out and found four long and relatively straight branches and made them into torches. Draig was delirious with fever, but they carried him outside and laid him into the wagon. Drakeson brought out his sword and shield, lying them down beside him.

Wilona and Drakeson climbed into the seat of the wagon as Myrddin lit the torches and handed one each to Coinchend, Thibalexis and Captain Arimah. They then began the procession to the circle of stones with Myrddin and Coinchend out in front of the wagon, while Thibalexis and Captain Arimah brought up the rear. There were also a few figures following along in the shadows as to remain unseen.

When they arrived at the circle of stones they stopped the cart outside and carried Draig into the center of the circle where they laid him on the ground. Those few figures that followed them at a distance had become a throng of several dozen by the time they arrived at the circle, and they were now much closer than before.

As they stood silent vigil over Draig, Myrddin took Draig's sword from the wagon. He stood in the circle of stones and, using the tip of the sword, he drew a pentagram on the ground and then stepped into it.

Tapping the sword three times at the north side of the pentagram, Myrddin spoke:

"Lugnasa, ruler of the northern dragons, I summon thee! Grant us your presence for this son of Man."

Tapping the sword three times at the east side of the pentagram, he spoke:

"Beltaine, ruler of the eastern dragons, I summon thee! Grant us your presence for this son of Man."

Tapping the sword three times at the south side of the pentagram, he spoke:

"Imbolic, ruler of the southern dragons, I summon thee! Grant us your presence for this son of Man."

Tapping the sword three times at the west side of the pentagram, he spoke:

"Samhain, ruler of the western dragons, I summon thee! Grant us your presence for this son of Man."

As Myrddin finished the ritual, orbs of light began to appear. First one and then another, one by one, the orbs appeared until the whole area was bathed in the light of a multitude of orbs of light. As they stood there in silence, a ghostly apparition approached. The vaguely formed spirit reached out and touched Draig.

"Draig, son of Anarcher, son of Eafa, son of Eoppa, I have come to you. Do you feel my presence?"

Draig opened his eyes, "Yes, I hear your words, but I am having trouble seeing you."

The ghostly apparition grew brighter and slowly began to take form. First, a large body formed, and then wings began to grow slowly out from the body. Moments later, the apparition sharpened until it took the form of a dragon in spirit form.

"Can you see me now, son of Man?" the spirit asked.

"Yes, Draco, I can see you better now. I have missed you, old friend."

The spirit of Draco spoke softly. "I am a part of you as you are a part of me. I promised you long ago that I would be with you for all the years of your life and beyond. I am here to fulfill that promise."

Three more ghostly apparitions approached. As did the first, these apparitions slowly grew brighter and began to take form. First, their bodies formed, and then wings began to grow slowly out from the bodies. After a moment, these apparitions sharpened until they took the form of dragons in spirit form. The three of them then stood near Draig.

The spirit of Draco spoke again. "Look, Draig, look who else has come to honor you."

"I see them!" Draig said, "I see them, Draco! Bellorus, Dormanus, Melkoran, my dear friends! I have not forgotten!"

The spirit of Bellorus spoke. "Yes, Draig, and because you kept our memories alive, they were able to reach into the in-between and pull our spirits out and bring us home. Because of your devotion to our memory, we are able to be here to honor you."

"We are not the only ones who have come," the spirit of Draco said. "Many have come to honor you, my friend. Look around you and see all who have come to honor you, Dragonrider!"

As Draig looked around the circle of stones, a great host of ghostly apparitions approached. Each in its own turn slowly grew brighter and began to take form. First a body formed, and then wings slowly grew from the body until they each became dragons in spirit form. They all stood at the edge of the circle just within the light given off by the orbs.

Draig gazed at all the dragons that had come and smiled as he scanned their many faces. He could not believe that so many had come to honor him. Just then, Draig's eyes met those of his wife and son.

He motioned to Drakeson and Wilona to come near. As Wilona reached Draig, she dropped to her knees and began to weep uncontrollably. Draig reached out and touched her arm. She continued to weep as Draig reached up and caressed her face with the palm of his hand.

"Do not weep for me, my wife, for I have lived more years than anyone could ever hope for, and I have spent the last of these years with the best wife in the whole world. What more could a man ask for? Remember me as I was and not as I am now."

Wilona placed her hand over his hand while it was still on her cheek. "I will always remember my husband. I will always remember the day you found me chained to a tree and bought my freedom. I will always remember the day you brought me here to make us one. I will always remember the day our son was born. And I will remember these days and more for as long as I live!"

Draig then turned his attention to Drakeson and with a forced smile said, "Drakeson, my son, do not mourn my death, but rather rejoice in the memories that are my life."

Thibalexis brought Draig his sword and shield. He laid the shield next to his side, placed his sword on his chest, and put the hilt in his trembling hands.

"Draig, here is your shield and sword so that your armor is complete," Thibalexis said.

Draig held the sword tightly in his hands and slowly reached down and ran his fingers across the runes engraved into the blade. He managed to smile, but it was for but a fleeting moment as he could not hold back a tear that flowed from his right eye.

"San ceum mar ri dragon," Drakeson said with a forced smile. "He walks with dragons."

"Take my sword, Drakeson," Draig said. "I will not need it where I am going."

Just then four ghostly apparitions emerged from the darkness. As they moved into the light of the orbs, they took the form of dragons in spirit form. They took positions around the circle at the north, south, east and west.

Thibalexis whispered to Drakeson, "Look! The four rulers have come to attend your father."

Thibalexis then pointed to each of them and called out their names, beginning at the north side: "Lugnasa, Samhain, Beltaine and Imbolic. They have all come to pay respect to your father."

"My father was that great a dragonrider?" Drakeson asked in a whisper.

"Yes, Drakeson," Thibalexis said. "He was such a great a dragonrider that all these great ruler dragons have come to honor him!"

Suddenly, another spirit appeared and descended. Its specter was much brighter than the others, and as it came near, it slowly took form and became a dragon in spirit form. Myrddin, Thibalexis and Coinchend all fixed their gaze upon this last spirit. They quickly recognized her, and each dropped to one knee.

"Great Mother, Tiamat!" they exclaimed in a single voice.

The spirit of Tiamat smiled at the trio, who continued to kneel before her. She then turned her attention to Draig. Reaching down and touching Draig ever so gently, she spoke:

"Draig, son of Anarcher, son of Eafa, son of Eoppa, I have come to honor you. One day, years ago, you sacrificed yourself so that dragonkind could survive. One day not long ago you sacrificed yourself so that the world of Man could survive. These sacrifices must not go unrewarded, dragonrider."

"Great Mother, my time here is done," Draig said. "I will miss my wife and my son, but I am ready to come home."

Draig closed his eyes and was gone. As the spirit of Draco stood over Draig's lifeless body, a single tear ran down his face. A silence followed that seemed to last forever. The silence was finally broken as the dragon spirits began to chant in some strange and unknown language. The four ruler dragons also began to chant, though it was obvious that they were chanting different words than the others.

It was then that a swirling mist rose up from the body of Draig. At first it simply hovered a few inches above his body. After a moment it slowly transformed into a sphere of translucent light. The sphere continued to hover above Draig's motionless body. After a few more minutes, the sphere rose slowly into the air until it finally faded from sight.

The ruler dragons switched their chanting to the same words the other dragons were chanting. Myrddin and Thibalexis then approached Draig's now lifeless body. As the dragon spirits continued to chant, Myrddin and Thibalexis removed Draig's armor and began to wrap him in white linen cloth.

As the dragon spirits continued to chant, the orbs of light began to swirl about, in and out of the stones. The orbs were moving to the cadence of the chanting, continuing to circle and absorbing one another, becoming fewer and fewer yet bigger and brighter. Eventually, there were but four large orbs sitting just outside the circle of stones, hovering in the north, east, south and west.

Beyond the chanting it was eerily still. There was not even the slightest breeze to cause the orbs of light to flicker against the background of the darkness that lay beyond them. It was as if, just for a moment, the whole world was collectively holding its breath in honor of Draig.

The spirit of Tiamat looked down at Draig's now lifeless body. She then reached out and touched Drakeson gently on his cheek.

"Draig was born of Man, but he lived his life as a dragon," she told Drakeson. "In combating the evil known as Saetan, he made the ultimate sacrifice. He is no longer a son of Man. He is now dragon. Know that your father is once again where he belongs—among dragonkind for all time."

The spirit of Tiamat then turned to Thibalexis and Myrddin, who again knelt before her. She moved toward them and touched each of them on the top of their heads. She then smiled and spoke to them:

"Thibalexis and Myrddin, you have not been forgotten either. And be certain that when your time comes we will come for you as well. If you cannot come to this place, let it be known that Coinchend will tell us when you approached the portal to the otherworld, and we will fetch you before you can pass beyond."

Thibalexis and Myrddin both thanked the spirit of Tiamat for the kind words. The spirit of Tiamat then turned to Coinchend. She smiled at her as she touched her on the cheek.

The spirit of Tiamat said, "Dear Coinchend, if you ever tire of living in the Otherworld, you are welcome to join us. This offer will remain open for all of eternity. All you have to do is ask and we will bring you to us."

"Thank you, Tiamat," said Coinchend. "I will remember your offer always."

One by one, the dragon spirits slowly moved away and disappeared. This continued until only the spirit of Draco remained. Draco then turned to Drakeson and placed a hand upon his shoulder.

"Drakeson, son of Draig, son of Anarcher, son of Eafa, stand and face me." As Drakeson stood before him, the spirit of Draco continued speaking. "As long as you remember him he is not truly gone. Remember him always."

Drakeson then knelt before his father. "I will remember you, my father, for as long as I live and beyond."

The spirit of Draco looked at Myrddin and spoke. "Myrddin, I sense your heavy heart. We know you did everything your knowledge permitted, but there is no cure for the darkness. Let go your pain least it consume you."

The spirit of Draco then looked at Thibalexis and said, "Thibalexis, we sent word that Draig needed your help and you came. You did what was expected of you. You can be proud of yourself as we too are proud of your actions."

The spirit of Draco looked to Coinchend and said, "Coinchend, warrior princess of the Otherworld, we thank you for leaving your world and coming here to help Draig. When you return to your home, you leave us not as a princess but as a queen."

The spirit of Draco then turned to Captain Arimah. "You came out of friendship for a man you knew for only two days. You paid Draig a great honor by your presence. May there always be wind in your sails and a calm sea to sail upon."

The spirit of Draco then disappeared. The figures that had been hidden in the shadows began to slowly move forward. As they came closer, those at the circle recognized that it was the Angeln who had come to watch the funeral for Draig.

As their faces became lit by the orbs, a look of confusion came over them. It was then that a dragon spirit, which had remained unnoticed until now, stepped forward. Upon seeing him, the Angeln dropped to their knees and hid their faces.

"Great Cinaed, you live!"

"Draig was my voice in this world," Cinaed said, "but his time here has ended. Honor his life as you honor me."

Cinaed looked to Myrddin and Thibalexis and winked. He then disappeared. The Angeln rose and slowly backed away. When they were beyond the light from the orbs, they scurried off to their village.

The orbs slowly dimmed and vanished. Captain Arimah and Thibalexis loaded Draig's cold body onto the cart, and they all returned to the farm. Wilona and Coinchend sat down on the stone bench under the oak tree as the men, by the light of their torches, took turns digging a grave between those of Lucky and Onyxia. Even Drakeson took his turn in the digging.

Once the grave was dug, Myrddin and Thibalexis took the wagon and collected some sandstone. They brought the sandstone back to the farm and placed part of it in the bottom of Draig's grave. They then laid him into the grave and covered him with the rest of the sandstone.

Myrddin brought his palms together and drew into his palms the energy of the treoir. He let the treoir form a ball of energy, and the ball of energy became an orb of fire. He then held the fiery orb in his hand and slowly released the fire into Draig's grave.

Slowly the sandstone changed from sandstone into quartzite. When Myrddin was done, it was as if Draig was encased in a giant clear crystal. Draig was now encased in a tomb that would be forever protected from the elements. They then covered his tomb over with dirt.

Myrddin and Drakeson then gathered a large stone from the river and brought it to the farm. Myrddin once again brought his palms together and drew into his palms the energy of the treoir. He let the treoir form a ball of energy, and the ball of energy became an orb of fire. Myrddin then took the orb of fire in his right hand and released small balls of fire which cut into the stone. Slowly, the stone became a carved headstone. At the top of the stone was *DRAIG* and below that were the words *San Ceum Mar Ri Dragon.*

There was a moment of silence, and then they started to head toward the house. Myrddin put his hand on Drakeson's shoulder and held him back as the others walked into the house. He then knelt before the boy and looked into his eyes.

"Face the oak tree and close your eyes," Myrddin said. "Think of your father and remember that he was from a time when what was, what is, and what shall be were all one in the same. Now open your eyes and behold!"

Drakeson opened his eyes, and what he saw brought a smile to his face. He saw four spirits standing under the oak tree. Before him stood his father sitting on Onyxia with Lucky at the front of the saddle, and Draco stood behind them with his wings spread wide.

Drakeson turned to speak to Myrddin, but he had disappeared. When he turned back and looked at the tree, the spirits were gone. Just then Drakeson heard the voice of his father:

"My sword and my armor are now yours. You are now Drakeson the dragonrider, san ceum mar ri dragon. Remember me always, my son."

"I will, Father. I promise."

Drakeson then took one last look at the three graves under the oak tree. After a moment, he turned and walked into the house and closed the door.

Early the next morning, Myrddin left the house for his trip home. Before heading home, he stopped at Draig's grave for a moment, and then he waved to his friends who were all standing by the house and walked away. They watched until he disappeared in the distance. At midday, Thibalexis and Captain Arimah bid their hosts good-bye as well. They walked to the oak tree and stood there in silence while looking at Draig's grave. Finally, they turned and headed south toward the coast. They regretted having to leave, but it was time that Captain Arimah returned to his ship, and Thibalexis had his own path to follow.

Not long after the men were gone it was Coinchend's turn. She reached out and hugged both Wilona and Drakeson and then kissed each of them on the cheek.

"I, too, must take my leave," Coinchend said. "It will soon be the Day of the Dead and time for me to return to my own realm. While there is still time, I wish to visit my old home before I have to return. Always remember that I am but a memory away. Think of me and I shall be there."

She then walked out of the door and disappeared. It was now just Wilona and Drakeson alone on the farm. For both of them the farm seemed terribly empty now, but they would have to get used to it. Drakeson finally decided to go out and do the chores while there was still enough daylight to do it.

While doing his chores, Drakeson looked up to see a party of men riding toward the farm. Drakeson counted fourteen men riding in two columns. There were six soldiers each at the front and rear, wearing swords at their sides and carrying lances with small banners waving in the wind. Between them was an older man, a nobleman dressed in fine silk clothes and a young boy riding at his side who was most likely the man's servant.

Drakeson ran to the house to alert his mother to the visitors. Wilona and Drakeson stood at the door as the group came closer. Finally the group stopped and the nobleman advanced alone.

The man called down from his horse: "I am Jerrod, Counselor to Queen Paula. I have come a great distance to see the man called Draig."

Wilona pointed toward the oak tree and said, "Sire, I am sorry to say that you have come one day too late."

The man climbed down off his horse and walked over to the graves and knelt. As he rose and stood looking at the tombstones, Wilona and Drakeson walked up and stood behind him.

Drakeson spoke softly to the man. "I am his son, Drakeson. This is my mother, Wilona. We buried him last night. You have missed him by just a few short hours."

"We met him on a road many years ago while Queen Paula was still a princess," Jerrod said. "He shared a meal with us and gave the princess a few gold coins."

Jerrod then walked over to his horse and fiddled in a saddle bag until he pulled out a small bag of coins. He walked back to Wilona and Drakeson and placed the bag in Drakeson's hand.

"The queen handed me this bag of coins and sent me to find your father. It is a simple reward for a simple kindness."

Jerrod then reached into his pocket and pulled out a small pouch. He opened the pouch and removed a large ring and handed it to Wilona.

Jerrod said, "Queen Paula made a decree. She has declared Draig a Minster of the Realm. This ring is the symbol of that position."

Jerrod then mounted his horse and returned to his men. Wilona and Drakeson watched as they rode away. Wilona then looked at the ring and saw that the ring bore the symbol of a falcon.

After dinner, Drakeson stood there looking at the bottle of wine as it sat on the shelf. He looked at his mother and then looked back at the bottle of wine. He looked to his mother once more, and then he took the bottle of wine from the shelf and walked out to the barn and climbed the stairs to the loft.

Drakeson placed the bottle down on the rings that were on the floor in front of the chest. He took a piece of wood and carved a plaque and carved the name "DRAIG" upon it. He then hung the plaque on the wall above the other plaques. He took the cup from behind the chest and filled it with wine, placing the bottle on the floor. He knelt on the floor and held up the cup.

"Bellorus, I drink to your memory!" And he took a sip from his cup.

"Dormanus, I drink to your memory!" And he took a sip from his cup.

"Melkoran, I drink to your memory!" And he took a sip from his cup.

"Draig, son of Anarcher, son of Eafa, son of Eoppa, I drink to your memory, my father!" And he took a sip from his cup.

Drakeson then sat down on the floor and refilled his cup. He pushed the cork back into the bottle and sat silently sipping his wine. The tradition had now passed to him from father to son.

As he neared the bottom of the cup, he stood up. Tears slowly rolled down his face as he relived past memories, not because they were sad memories, but because there was no longer anyone with whom to share them.

With that, he drank the last of the wine in his cup. He placed the cup back behind the chest and put his hands on the large chest and called out:

"And what now, Father? What is it that I do now that you are gone? Who will teach me what you have not had time to teach?"

Drakeson knelt before the chest and reached for the bottle of wine when suddenly the loft began to grow brighter. He was startled by a voice that came from behind him.

"Rise, son of Man. Close your eyes and prepare."

Drakeson turned his head to see a dragon spirit standing at the back of the loft. While he was surprised at first, he was now curious as to whom this spirit belonged. Drakeson stood and looked at the dragon spirit for a moment.

"Who are you?" Drakeson asked.

"Drakeson, son of Draig, son of Anarcher, son of Eafa, close your eyes and prepare."

Drakeson closed his eyes. He felt a hand on his chest. At first it was just a warm feeling, but the warmth grew hotter. Soon Drakeson felt as if there was a fire burning within his chest. Draco spoke in some mystical tongue that Drakeson could feel to the very core of his being. A voice boomed out that seemed to come from everywhere at once:

"We are the Great Ones of your ancestors!"

Drakeson dropped to his knees, feeling totally drained. As he opened his eyes, the burning in his chest began to fade. Drakeson then looked down at his chest expecting it to be burned, but there was no mark whatsoever.

"Drakeson, son of Draig, son of Anarcher, son of Eafa, hear my words and remember. As it was with your father, so it is with you. I have placed a small piece of myself within you. Wherest you go for all the days of your life and beyond, I shall be there too."

"Who will teach me now that my father is gone?" Drakeson asked.

"You have already learned well the lessons of your father. You are already a dragonrider in the eyes of dragonkind, but I will teach you those things you have not yet learned."

Drakeson asked, "When will I learn the magic of the dragons like my father?"

"When it is time, you shall learn to channel the great power of the Great Ones. For now, comfort thy mother because her loss is great."

The spirit of Draco then faded away and the loft grew dim. Drakeson reached down and picked up the bottle of wine. Slowly, he looked around the dimly lit loft. He felt as if his father's spirit was standing there looking at him, but he saw nothing.

When he walked into the house, he saw his mother sitting near the fireplace. She turned to him and forced a smile. Drakeson placed the bottle back on the shelf and gave his mother a hug. He then sat down in his father's chair.

Bonus Poems

    The following poems have been added for your reading pleasure. Some may ask why I included them. If you have read the first book of the series, you would have seen that I included poems, the first of which was the premise of the book. The others were incorporated into the book as well.

    These poems are related to that facet of Draig's life that he was not allowed to express. If you have read the first book, you may have an understanding of why he was not allowed. If you have not read the first book, you may or may not understand why these poems were added; however, they are still here for your enjoyment.

The Mountain

I climb a nearby mountain, until the air is cold and thin;

And seek a place where I can sit, where no other man has been.

I close my eyes, take a breath, and reach beyond my mind;

Only one answer do I seek, but I cannot seem to find.

I sit here in my solitude, in this place where nothing's said,

Till the clear blue sky grows dark, and the stars are overhead.

I do not ask for riches, and I cannot tell you why;

I only seek to love, and to be loved, just once before I die.

Perhaps I ask too much, though I really don't know how;

But it is much too late to ask again, so I must go for now.

As I prepare to leave my mountain, the place I hide my fears,

I know it is that time again, to wipe away my tears.

But before I leave my secret place, where it often snows,

Just in case I'm not the only one, I leave a single rose.

The Dream

I close my eyes, and drift away to another time and place.

Shades of gray on shades of gray, shadows on top of shadows.

Through the varied shades of darkness, I see light upon your face.

My soul mate or my guardian, only Destiny really knows.

I stand before the winds of time, a forgotten uncharted sea,

And yearn to feel your presence, though we stand so far apart.

I reach beyond my mind, beyond this vessel I call me;

I cross the swirling mist called Fate, I open up my heart.

I feel the rush of Truth, what is and what shall be,

Beyond my fringe of knowledge, like ribbons in the wind;

The paths of Life are many, but only one shall I yet see,

For they are but the branches of a tree that cannot bend.

The hours pass in minutes, the dark gives way to light.

That which first drew me here, slowly pushes me away.

I now return from whence I came, no chance is there to fight,

For it is now that time again to live another day.

Made in the USA
Columbia, SC
06 December 2022